UN NUEVO SOL

British LatinX Writers

edited by Nathalie Teitler
y Nii Ayikwei Parkes

flipped eye publishing
london

Un Nuevo Sol: British LatinX Writers

First published in 2019 by flipped eye publishing

A version of Maia Elsner's *Transnational Zoo* also appears
in the Summer 2019 edition of *Blackbox Manifold*.
Versions of Juana Adcock's poems in this anthology also
appear in her collection *Split* (Blue Diode, 2019)'

This book is typeset in Century Gothic and
Palatino from Linotype GmbH

flipped eye publishing
www.flippedeye.net

ISBN: 978-1905233564

UN NUEVO SOL

PRAISE FOR ***UN NUEVO SOL***

THE ANTHOLOGY 'UN Nuevo Sol' magnifies the wilful invisibility of a distinct minority group by the powerful act of 'Naming' – Latinx. This gathering and sampling of contemporary British Latinx poets, fiction and theatre writers is therefore both trailblazing and an act of literary activism. We witness a community not only in conversation with a long history of Latin American literature and each other, but dialoguing with African American and Black British Literature, creating rich and exciting work that is so necessary. We are exposed to a new generation of bold and audacious multilingual writers who are experimental, playful and non-linear. Writers rightfully pushing the boundaries of literary practise thereby complicating and expanding the British canon, continuing a postcolonial history of the margin challenging the status quo and enriching 'British literature'.

The uniqueness of this anthology is not only the ruthless interrogation by these activist writers of: personal identity, gender roles and Queer narratives, but an earnest impulse to grapple with multilingual concerns and find literary strategies to evoke the complications of language.

Yet it is arguably the distinctiveness of these ten writers in their individual experimentation with language and silence, with shape and versification, haunting elegies and feminist fairytales, with non-linear narratives and the surreal lyric, with fractured dramatic monologues and revealing memoir, with diary entries and syncopated text, with vulnerable characters and confessional verse, but most importantly with the risks each has taken with the black ink and white space on the page, that makes this an important significant inaugural anthology that is long overdue.

Malika Booker

author of ***Pepper Seed****, Cholmondeley Award Winner and former Poet-in-Residence at the Royal Shakespeare Company*

Not many books are necessary, but this anthology of poetry and prose that falls into that liminal category. Katherine's poem flirt deftly with metaphor and metonymy, Gaël's play extract holds its tension not only in what is happening, but in our struggle to sense what is happening, Luiza's short story on queer love shudders with familiarity and nostalgia and Karina's story, about an old racist, who builds a fortress around himself and dies, who is shown the greatest kindness when nature comes to reclaim him, is precious with its humanity and understanding. Not only are these voices from Argentina to Brazil, Bolivia to Mexico, important to broadening and deepening the British literary cannon, they prove that we have ignored them for too long and to our own detriment. These are precise and luminous writers and this is a precise and luminous book.

Inua Ellams

author of ***Candy-Coated Unicorns and Converse All Stars****,* ***The Half-God of Rainfall*** *and* ***The Barbershop Chronicles***

In such divisive times as these it has never been more important to look outside narrow perspectives and search for the nuance in things. This anthology, focusing as it does on the work, illuminates a few examples from a thrillingly various corpus of writing by British LatinX writers that is yet to be properly appreciated. This anthology begins, or better to say reignites, a needful discussion about the hybrid multilingual nature of the UK and the failure of literary culture to recognize that breadth and its generative possibilities. May its publication lay down a challenge to editors, writers, readers, booksellers, and programmers to read and celebrate a wider span of anglophone literature especially that which reveals the porous boundaries between languages in our contemporary moment

Kayo Chingonyi

author of ***Kumukanda*** *and winner of the Dylan Thomas Award*

This remarkable anthology does what art should do: coax us out of our comfort zones. I've been conceptualizing "Latinx literature" as solely anchored in the Americas. This volume confirms how parochial my thinking has been—it's a welcome and overdue gift.

Francisco Aragón

author of ***After Rubén*** *and editor of* ***The Wind Shifts: New Latino Poetry***

TABLE OF CONTENTS

INTRODUCTION

UN NUEVO SOL is the first major anthology of British Latinx writers to be published. It includes ten writers, some born in the UK with mixed British/Latin heritage, others who came to Britain at a later stage in life and made it their home. They represent the worlds of fiction, poetry and theatre and come from a wide range of countries and places including: Argentina, Mexico, Brazil, Peru, the Amazon, Scotland, Ireland and England. Prior to this anthology, they had all been writing in almost complete isolation, unaware of each other's existence. In spite of this, there are many common threads that run through their work: the experimental nature, playfulness around language (Spanish/English/Spanglish), use of coding/silence, focus on storytelling, rich imagery and the refusal to use Western tropes of linear time or exist in a reality of only five senses. All of these things can be found in Latin American literature and make the voice of British Latinx writers one that both adds to the traditional British Canon and interrogates it. This interrogation is deliberate and speaks to another point of commonality: all of the writers have activist backgrounds, again something that is rooted in their Latin American origins where the worlds of politics and literature are far more closely linked than is usual in the UK.

This activism was also behind the choice of the term British Latinx. As in the United States, the terminology around Latin Americans living in diaspora is hotly debated. These writers selected the term 'Latinx' because of its refusal to allow the gender binary implicit in Latino/a. The 'X' can be seen as a symbol of resistance, not only to gender binaries but also to race binaries. Latin Americans outside of their continent exist in a liminal space somewhere between black and white, between Spanish/Portuguese and English. The tensions created act as both a challenge and a creative incentive. An incentive to write themselves into existence and allow their voice to be heard on mainstream UK/international literature platforms. This is the force that drives their writing and was the main force behind creating this anthology.

As with most things Latin American and British Latinx, however, the genesis of this anthology is both political and highly personal. In fact, the story of this anthology begins almost five decades ago in the early 1970s when I was born in a hospital in Recoleta, a leafy wide-avenued district of Buenos Aires. The same hospital where Eva Peron died decades earlier. My time in Argentina was short, when I was still a small infant my mother took me to have a professional photograph taken. This was to be added to her passport so that we could travel. The picture shows a scrawny, and distinctly grumpy, baby with a tuft of almost black hair on an otherwise bald head. My mother had tied a large pink bow on to my hair. She had probably hoped it would improve my appearance (it did not), or at least identify me as a girl child. She had refused to have my ears pierced, as is the custom in Latin countries. So it was that at the age of a few months I boarded a boat bound for England with my mother, father and older sister (then two). This was not unusual; the 1970s was a time of enormous political instability in many Latin American countries; waves of Chileans and Argentinians came to the UK seeking to escape dictatorships and disappearances. They were drawn, no doubt, by an idea of British democracy that seemed to offer a better life. In the years that followed they were joined by Nicaraguans, Cubans, a large influx of Colombians and more recently, Venezuelans. They became the foundation of what is now the British Latinx population. The 8th largest population in London and the fastest growing, with 2nd and 3rd generation members – children who were born and raised in the UK. In spite of the size of the community – approximately the same size as the British Asian population in 1991 – they are not acknowledged on any census, in schools or by funding organisations. This book is an attempt to begin to claim an identity; to be named. To be present.

My own story continues in London; we arrived to a freezing and grey British Winter. My mother claims that my sister and I suffered from a series of colds and flus that lasted for the remainder of our childhood: our bodies never adjusted. I did not return to Latin America during this time but something remained with me, perhaps something I had absorbed with the dulce de leche added to my milk and the Mercedes Sosa songs played at home. We spoke Spanish at home but I was aware of my own clumsiness in the language; a situation that meant I hardly ever spoke it in public. I gained a distinctly mainland Spanish accent after studying the language at school: as a result, when I did finally return to Argentina I was called 'the Spanish girl'. Throughout my childhood I found myself irresistibly drawn to Latin American culture; the music, the dance, the activism and – most of all-the literature. From Garcia Marquez through Bolaño to Clarice Lispector, here was a world in which magic realism combined with non-linear time and an abundant sensuality which took my breath away. I fell in love with a culture that believed poetry had breathed the world into being. A culture in which Quechua peoples told stories through qipos, intricate knots tied in incredibly complex weavings. In this world storytelling, politics and real life were woven together inextricably; something that felt 'right' in a way I could not explain.

At the age of 24 I went on to begin a PhD in Argentine women poets while continuing the activism I had been involved with from the age of 13. This was also when I started my first 'real' job. I say real to distinguish it from the early morning shifts at the Canadian Muffin company, and other student style employment of earlier years. The job was at a refugee community organisation in Bethnal Green, called Praxis, and I was assigned to the Latin American section. It was one of the few places to offer support to the British Latinx community at this time. My boss, Rosario L., was an activist from Nicaragua with a fierce intellect and a huge amount of energy; when she left I took over her position. We helped Latin American women find housing, set up small businesses, learn English and get counselling/support for domestic abuse. My favourite part of the job, however, was the work with the young people which involved assisting with arts projects. I was lucky enough to work with a Colombian lawyer/activist Laura Villegas, at IRMO (Indo-American Refugee and Migrant Organisation), who had set up the first bi-lingual young peoples' theatre group. It was Laura who decided that I was perfectly suited to teaching the young people creative writing in Spanish and English. A decision – more of a leap of faith – that was to have a huge impact on my career. It was then that I met Marta: a young Afro-Colombian girl of fifteen who wrote with searing honesty and extraordinary imagery about the violence- and also the vibrant colour- in the life she had left behind. When I first read her work it was as if my body responded with a rush of adrenaline. I knew her writing was special. I began to make plans for her: to go to Oxford on a scholarship, to get published. All of these plans came to a halt when Marta's mother and father went to a parents' evening at their daughter's school. They were told that – in spite of her 'A' grades – Marta would not be suited to further education and should pursue a career as a hairdresser. I later found out that this was the same message given to every single Latin American child at that time, particularly those with any trace of an accent. Marta dropped out of the youth group and I never saw her again.

What followed was 25 years of teaching creative writing and nurturing and developing writers, with a focus on those who wrote from the position of 'other'. Not because of any desire to tick arbitrary boxes but because I found these voices, these versions of the world, so much more exciting than those offered by more mainstream writers. I worked for a three- way project for Refugee Action, the Home Office and Arts Council England and founded the first mentoring and translation scheme for writers living in exile. Later I became director of an organisation called the Complete Works Poetry, promoting diversity in UK poetry. I was lucky, it was a good time to embark on promoting inclusivity in the arts. The British Latinx community continued to grow during this time, setting up numerous bi-lingual newspapers, shopping areas, restaurants and a Carnival reaching hundreds of thousands. In spite of this, in all my years of promoting inclusivity I did not come across a single British Latinx writer at a mainstream literature festival/event in the UK. At events promoting diversity in literature I would bring this up to people I believed were allies, their response was disappointing; 'Aren't they going to go home?', 'Do they know how to write in English?' or even 'I doubt there any writers'. As Latin America is a continent that has given birth to more Nobel literature prize winners than any other, I found it unlikely that the entire population had lost all ability to write fiction on arrival in the United Kingdom. As I fought for representation for BAME and LGBTQ writers, I became increasingly aware of a feeling of deep unease: I did not feel represented myself. I was uncomfortably aware that people were talking to a version of me that had little relationship to my inner bi-lingual and multi-cultural voice; a voice that was heavily influenced by my relationship with Latin America.

In 2017 I had the great good fortune of meeting the Argentinian poet/international journalist Leo Boix who was a member of the Complete Works Poetry. Leo had lived in Britain for 20 years and was as passionate about British Latinx representation and literature as I was. Having published two successful collections in Latin America, he was now perfecting a different voice and style in his English poetry, making him a truly bi-lingual poet. In other words, the perfect person for me to work with; it is not an exaggeration to say this anthology would not exist without him. In 2018 we were given funding by Arts Council England to start a project, Invisible Presence, to find, nurture and develop British Latinx writers. The process of outreach was- as anticipated- not easy. I asked the many people I knew in key UK literature organisations if they could point me too any British based writers of Latin American background. The answer was a unanimous 'no', usually accompanied by a quizzical raised eyebrow to suggest the question was irrelevant. Of even greater concern, I spoke to the many writers I knew working in schools, for SLAMS and other literature projects. I knew that the percentage of British Latinx kids in London schools was high-with some schools having at least 70% Latin population. I was truly dispirited to find the answer to my question of whether they had any British Latinx children of talent was 'No, we've never had any'. There were two things that worried me about this: the first was that there was absolutely no concern over the fact that such a significant group – representing an entire continent – was not deemed worthy enough of attention for their absence to be remarked. The second was that I knew this statement to be untrue: I had attended SLAM sessions where there were British Latinx young people. The tutors had simply assigned them the labels of 'White-other' or 'Black-other' depending on their skin tone (Latinidad covers the full gamut of skin tones, with frequent visible markers of Quechua identity). They were expected to write within the framework of whichever culture they had – wrongly-been assigned to. With their own culture completely denied and limited to the English language, these young people did not thrive. At Black History Month events around the country there was never any mention of Latin American culture or history. Leo reported that when he began a residency at a London school with a 70% of British Latinx children, they had been moved to tears when he began to read. This was not just due to the fact that his poetry is fierce, but was also because that they had never heard anyone with a Latin American accent read at their school, or had any aspect of their Latin American heritage being celebrated in this space. I was deeply upset by this: the story of Marta seemed to be repeating itself without any sign of improvement.

I followed the fights to keep Latin Village open, the fierce Union of women cleaners campaigning for their rights, heard of frequent racist attacks that went unreported and realised that this was linked to the fact that British Latinx remains unnamed on any census. Why does this matter? For the children of this group, many of them born in this country, this absence causes significant damage: neither 'white-other' nor 'black-other' they become a symbol of unnameable-and therefore-unresolvable 'otherness'. Culturally, linguistically and often visibly distinct, they become a target for race based attacks from all sides. Attacks that are often not identified as 'racial' because they have yet to be acknowledged as actually belonging to a race. Representation becomes impossible when your racial background has yet to be granted a formal name and status. To be British Latinx is to live the experience of constantly translating yourself on all levels; to be accustomed to people addressing a version of you that bears little resemblance to your actual identity. It is to know what it means to be both present and invisible.

After a significant amount of time placing bi-lingual flyers around Elephant and Castle, trekking around Brixton eating empanadas and discussing bachata and salsa with an impressive number of the British Latinx community (*'yes, salsa dura es lo mejor', 'Maluma es realmente un 'pretty boy', 'claro que Shakira dances mejor que Beyonce'*), Leo and I eventually found ten writers for Invisible Presence. Ten writers who represented a huge range of Latin American countries as well as England, Scotland and Wales in an extraordinary variety of combinations; the true British Latinx community. The project culminated in a showcase at the Roundhouse in November

2018 that I will never forget. The first reason was because of the increasing panic of the Roundhouse staff as we had only sold about 20 of 200 tickets a few hours before the show. I assured them that this was not a problem; Latin people and time work in mysterious ways, or at least mysterious to British culture. Sure enough, the show was sold out and the Roundhouse reported it was the first time they had ever sold the majority of tickets to an event twenty minutes **after** it started. The second – and more important – reason that I will never forget it has more to do with the audience response. It was a truly multi-lingual evening with writers moving smoothly from Spanish to English through Spanglish (now being researched at Queen Mary's University as a separate language) with some Portuguese and Quechua. The audience did not miss a beat; from shouts of 'arriba' to the intense finger clicking and feet stamping associated with the spoken word scene (and some specifically Latin shouting and dancing in seats which has to be experienced to be understood). This was an entire audience of people who were breathing a huge sigh of relief because finally, finally they were represented. The voice in their heads was the same as the one on stage; the identity that they had felt would never be publically acknowledged was being celebrated on a mainstream platform. The evening was a huge success and culminated in my leading a group Reggaeton – and the Roundhouse staff trying to get a very rowdy, tearful and joyous crowd out of their building.

It was a moment of epiphany for me as I realised that the British Latinx voice was one which could enrich British literature immeasurably and that there was an imperative to share it, to promote it for the sake of the community – particularly the young people growing up feeling they were not acknowledged or represented. During the course of the Invisible Programme, Leo and I had discovered an increasing number of British Latinx writers – writers teaching at Universities, writers who had published widely, writers of great talent. Almost all of them were unaware of the other's existence; each one had thought they were alone. It was obvious to me that there was a very special anthology that needed to be created. I thought long and hard about who might be the right publisher for this; the answer was obvious. The independent publishing house flipped eye, founded by exceptional poet/writer Nii Ayikwei Parkes, had been doing extraordinary work promoting an incredibly diverse range of writers and poets for many years. The first to publish poets such as Warsan Shire, and Inua Ellams, I knew that their founder also had a real passion for Latin American literature and culture.

This anthology is the result of years of frustration and invisibility for British Latinx writers and the community. It contains exceptional novelists and poets at different stages of their careers. Their work is both complex and accessible, it moves through Spanish-Portuguese-English-Spanglish, it is magic realist and contemporary. It is political, passionate and populist. In other words, it is distinctly Latin American with a unique touch of British. I hope that it reaches the wide range of readers it deserves and that they enjoy this exciting new voice. I also pray that it reaches as many members of the British Latinx population as possible-particularly the young people. For all those Martas who are still being told you should not write, you cannot write, you cannot be represented, I hope this anthology counters with an undeniable, 'Si, se puede'. 'Yes, you can'.

Nathalie Teitler

LEO BOIX

BAUTISMO

Your baptism was *una estafa*. You had large scales
instead of pink skin. Your honeyed eyes stung
even under church's marble-painted font.
Priest wore strict black, your family congregated
for the grand occasion. As ceremony started
your head grew bigger, wider, your black tongue flew
in all directions. You had a dress made of fibreglass.
There wasn't even a full submersion. *El cuerpo seco.*
Aunt Susi told the story. They put you down
on a chequered floor, called 75 ageing Sisters
of the Discalced Carmelites, who in turn
gave you rose water, *aceite de romero*, rubbed you
in pig's fat all over, thrice prayed for your soul,
until you calmed down, & all went back to normal.

TRIPTYCH

I embarked
on a ship
of fools, landed
without words
to give away
tokens
unsolicited
look at
my hands
as I try
to trick you
into this
folly
…
I eat
inside
a barrel
this feast
not for me
lets devour
until
all's lost.
My pork's pie.

I, prodigal
son
instead
return
unrepentant
my rucksack
in the shape of
a snail—
este caracol
this going
round & round
this way
always
back
to a place
never there
where do you come
from?
you wanderer
invader
waving
to say
esta patria no es mía

By the time
they told me
he had a week
I disguised
myself
as a skeleton
with an arrow
on my hand.
Hello, dad!
hola papá
Your time's
up.
I
down there
disguised
as
monsieur
le mort
Your
time
is up!
I, & my
empty mouth.

SWALLOW

You are not a good omen
I will turn into a spirit
so I can return
home once more
& heal you
from recklessness
you told me once to leave but were wrong
lied in the shape of an apple a red lion
the things I did to mimic you the risks I took I spoke *like* you
my true omen
I'll follow you wherever you hide

THE SWAMP

When it rains here it reminds me
of vast muddy fields left untouched,
cows swimming, submarine giant ants.
Cleaning dark water brings death
to that fallen garden of Eden, fallen
lilac plumes dissolved in the ground,
crushed moths of our silent house in
Quilmes as toxic rain marked again
a new season of *tortas fritas*, cakes
cooked without oil, hot frothed *maté*
waiting for us in silence. Flooding
did come later, while a large herd
of stray dogs drowned in sewers
howling in Spanish, slippery tomb-
stones submerged, their letters vanished
in a deluge for mown English lawns.
I watch this sacred renewal in reverse,
a southern red crab going backwards
to its rockpool refuge hide, constantly
replenished, fully crystallised. It rains.
This unholy place reverts to its nature.
Earth drinks what's left, some *ranchos*,
a shoe, waterways to feed its dead.

ALCHEMIST'S FURNACE

"Sometimes they put me on to the torture table and stretched me out, tying my hands and feet to a machine which I can't describe since I never saw it, but which gave me the feeling that they were going to tear part of my body off." Testimony of Dr Norberto Liwsky (file No. 7397). Nunca Más (Never Again)-Report of Conadep - 1984

They pulled a hay wagon, cursed the world all the way
to their heavenly downfall. On horseback, crawling,
limping on one foot. Let them taste grass at all costs.

Popes, priests, *dictadores* follow a mad procession.
Hay to enrich them, to fall in love, climbing higher
to see demons above. Five Senses, Seven Sins.

Four elements for a world governed by fodder power.
A slow dance begins to unravel. Time for wild beasts.
Then, a carefully choreographed summit of half-animals.

In a desperate burning tower, naked men on stumps,
bodies decomposing. This a party of the disappeared.
Gone their hay wagon. And they fell down like toads.

JUDGEMENT

It won't be easy to enter the house of Hell
you will have to ask for permission, you

burn inside, fire in your eyes. An angry owl
guards the entrance. Frogs decorate a door

to the underworld. Don't scream yet, wait:
Your sins blindfolded, a sword on your chest.

Your wife calls a priest for the extreme unction.
You swallow words behind an armchair.

Hellish dreams for a dance that begins.
You sing: *Judgment is upon this world.*

Priest moves in a perfect circle.
You sing: *Have mercy upon us.*

An arrow stuck on your bloodied head.
You seem dead, mouth, eyes wide open.

Still fire grows inside. A simple brush
of bright yellow, red, glowing magenta.

GHAZAL: UN PASO AL COSTADO (A SIDE STEP)

Your feet, a rhythm of the flesh, as it pleases. A side step,
quick, slow, quick. Three forward strides, *un paso al costado,*

then a dragged one. Deer legs closing without changing weight.
A congregation before music begins, crossing *un paso al costado*.

Slow, slow. Forward with your left. You can smell fruit
decomposing, forest birds, feet intertwined, *un paso al costado*.

Swan necks contorted, touched by velvety hands. Slow, quick,
forward with your right. Wicked sighs, *un paso al costado.*

A rehearsal, *una fiesta* you are invited to. Come, come
join this reunion. *Salón de Tango*. Quick, *un paso al costado.*

Wild flowers stomped in Argentina, giant seed pods in jars,
a tango singer marks the rhythm for *un paso al costado.*

You look to naked bodies moving, a *comparsa*, they touch
before being executed. Blindfolded. Then, *un paso al costado.*

Slaughterhouse. Dance ended near Río de la Plata.
He, a Bosch-squid sucking all oxygen. *Un paso al costado.*

SAINT JEROME

He prayed as you did, dead-like
to whom, one wonders, *for what?*
  your bed, a simple stone made
imperfect. *Lower it son,*
    make pain go away, leave now. A cry,
wide landscape, in green tones.

  Like his, your red robes abandoned,
a straw hat by a pool's edge, Lethe. You—
a reflection that never came
back.

You prayed, unbeliever.
  Your dog wouldn't leave, he licked
your drying sutures. Thinner—
a twisted twig of the tree we planted.

Unceremoniously, at once
  wind-stopped.

   In a pond nearby,
a peel of dried fruit went adrift,
a plastic duck concealed inside.
            He sensed your death.

On an island this side of our bridge,
a little dead bird reappeared. Perhaps a lion—
Saint's companion- *leo* looking at you
from the bank.

Tame feline, flower-like, always out of place.

Lower the bed, son, further
                    make pain go.

Birds, -your favourites-, sang at your funeral.
                    Lying, face down
on the ground, enriching soil for *limoneros.*

Beyond this rocky place, a winding river, an unused church,
a farm you visited before I was born.
From an upper branch
a *venteveo* calls your name.
Later he'll be devoured by fire.

When the priest came round, you told your fears.
We left your makeshift room, like little insects
crawling to our hides…

UN VIAJE

Mother and I went on a cruise together—an ocean liner in the grand style. An old warship
full of suitcases, terracota pots with *retama* trees in flower, her favourites, a black headed ibis
its naked
neck
its down-curved
beak
The ship left Buenos Aires at night. We saw the white obelisk flickering. Mother looked out
from a porthole, towards the river mouth opening up. The wait had ended. Her final adieu as fast
as a blink,
a
split
second
She sat near the bird, told him of how her immigrants parents met during carnival as harlequin and Columbine. Of how she played Beethoven from a borrowed piano, later her measured sarcophagus.
It rained
eventually.
Stopped,
rained again.

Ours was a short trip. Not from A to B. More obliquely, in sections, a big undulating line stretching perilously. She forecasted disaster while looking

at her own reflection
in a mirror
(this I remember)
& her sadness for departing.

Then spoke of her childhood memories at *Costa Bonita,* its desolate landscape, mollusks full, seaweed wigs. Her endless walks at midday towards a sunken hulk, eaten by red crabs. Rusty edges and its

creatures, too
small, too
dependent
on incoming tides.

On board our ship, Mother knitted endlessly, sang with her soft voice. She moved her fingers quickly, made long multicoloured scarves, kept counting the rows, old stitches. On a wicker basket:

her knitting
needles
her ball
of frayed wool

We picked up speed, faster by the minute. Our destination in sight. I used binoculars to catch a glimpse, our *tierra prometida.* A mound with no tress, only sand, rocks. She wanted to say things, *quickly mother, say them before disembarking.*

A tongue
entangled
salty wind
seabirds ate

from her elegant hands. She had a blue satin dress chosen by

me for her. Sun set quicker, lower.
A sudden pink sky. *Look up,* mother.
A second
in motion
above cirrus
unmovable
Suddenly, our cruise ship hit a submerged sandbank, it cracked
from side to side
commotion aboard.
Mother thrown
overboard, still trying
to tell her story. *Look up, Mother.* Her delicate voice babbling underwater.

HELIOTROPE

After Ovid

—Reassigned body:
a desertion of
/he looks for clues/on his skin
answers denied/love's mouth shut, too.

—Under an open Argentinean sky/
he sat dishevelled
/bareheaded/bare-feet
/on bare earth.

—He only gazed/at God's Third Eye/
as he passed
/turned his transitioning face
/towards it.

—They say his soft limbs clung/
to the polluted soil
/his ghastly pallor
changed into flower/*una flor*

(a violet rosette hid his opened face)

—She turns, always/
        /to an exploded sun,
                /her roots hold her down,
/she's been altered.

KATHERINE LOCKTON

MI LENGUA

for Rosemary

Mientras comia mi cereal esta mañana
While eating my cereal this morning
se cayo mi lengua en mi plato. Se quedo ahí
my tongue fell off into my plate. It stayed there
nadando en la leche mientras mi mama me hablaba.
swimming in milk while my mum spoke.
No he podido decirle que no puedo hablar.
I couldn't tell her that I could no longer speak.
En ese momento lluegue a entender que la vida
In that moment I understood life
pasa mientras que nosotras las mujeres planchamos
passes us by while we the women iron
las camisas de nuestros hombres.
the shirts of our men.

AFTER RUBIX

Red:

'Look how he steps on birds' wings' they say,
'how he grabs at their feathers and makes
them his. If he falls it will be onto their backs'.

'We don't know our own bodies. I feel for my
thigh and find your calf, then her hip and his nose.
My thigh is lost somewhere between our bodies.'

They put him in a house too small for him.
Its walls push against his ears. This is
what they had said would happen if he lied.

What Red Does:

Our aunt sits us on giant chairs and tells us to stay.
We mustn't, we shouldn't, we can't and if we do.
The tomatoes sit on their shelf untouched but bruised.

We push him in a pram too big for us to hold,
our arms grabbing only the wheels. This is what
it is to love, my mother tells us; to push and push.

He doesn't know why he leans on this gate so much.
He only knows he fed the chickens here once, his
feet thick with mud. Sandra, his wife calling calling.

What Our Parents Don't Say About Red:

They painted bits of themselves red just to
feel the paint against them. It peeled off that very
night but they had felt what it was to be free.

When they no longer had a use for Miss X, they
turned her into a bike; her rear became a seat;
her neck; handles; fitted wheels onto her calves.

They planted us head down, stuck us as deep
as their hands could carve into mud and rock.
They didn't know we were weeds.

Yellow:

We bloomed in that nightly silence, danced
in its darkness. When they lit that match,
we had no use for its yellow beam.

The redness of their dance was all
we felt. Their blurred bodies moving
and moving until all we felt was them.

She threaded stones into her corset till
she could no longer move and waited.
Potatoes turned green on their shelves.

What Yellow Does:

It lay on its belly, broken. The world
seemed bathed in white light. The only one
of its kind made like this; made to break.

The day they wed, her mum threw birdseed
at their heads for luck. When the seeds fell
nearby pigeons came; eyes wide with hunger.

They hung the foal's mother, her head bowed;
as if she somehow knew to stay silent.
The men stood around in batches pointing.

What Our Parents Don't Say About Yellow:

The newborn bairns are in cots lined up
against blue walls, hello kitties painted
onto their feet. Outside it is raining still.

They are wearing huge glittery condoms
on their skulls and walking across fifth avenue
like this. They are praying, they say.

She blows bubbles as big as wild bears,
dancing to music only she hears. This time, this time,
they will take her away, her neighbours say.

Blue:

We cover our breasts in bees. The yellow
of them comforts us. They sting as they
try to suckle milk never meant for them.

With blunt scissors she chops away at the part of her
that loves him still. Her hair gone,
she contemplates cutting away at the rest.

While waiting for him to come home, she lays
herself out the way others lay out linen.
Her arms, legs, chest all neatly folded.

What Blue Does:

When I find that one of me is not enough.
I print eleven other versions just to
see if any number of me will ever be.

Our mother won't let us play with the neighbourhood
squirrels. Their fur is too thick, their legs
too thin. So she sends us to the sea.

The pigeons steal the newly wed couple
in their sleep, take them above clouds
never meant for the young and drop them.

What Our Parents Don't Say About Blue:

To cigarette in the city is to laugh, mouth wide
with candy: to stare into your loved one's
eyes as they smooth you down.

Her shadow still shows the missing bits of her.
The ones she put in a washing machine
just to be rid of the smell of herself.

He puts himself into a bottle for her. At six foot
two his feet stick out. The way they always did
in bed. She uses his shoes to push him down.

Green

We lie in bed as close as dominoes, ball bearings
digging into our hips. This is what it's like
to lose you over and over again.

You have taken my bed and spread your golden locks
across my pillow. The porridge I make for you
is too hot, too cold and never just right.

I dreamt you were amongst the stars,
your reflection falling into waves. My body pressed
against your light, as I fumbled the water's darkness.

What Green Does

The shed you build in your garden
is wonky, the door skewing to one side.
All I want to do is to live inside its walls.

You turn me over like an avocado past its best.
I am the bride who became frightened of life opening
before her eyes. My flesh no longer mine.

You carve yourself into my body. I watch from the ceiling.
I watch myself watching myself looking at us,
the two mes, the one before you and the one after.

What Our Parents Don't Say About Green

I am drawing a line between us in bed.
The marker fades as I press down into the sheets.
You tell me that there never will be another pen,

that this too is the last of the ink, and that I must make do,
before turning my hand away, and scrunching it into a fist.
When I can't sleep I give Selima's men breasts.

I dress them in my old leotards. They arch their backs,
but do not fall into her water. Instead they bend
themselves back onto spikes and laugh.

Orange

You make prints of my breasts,
hand them out to your friends. This is only to be expected,
your wife says, slamming your door on me.

I give you a box you can't refuse, but the paper is too tight.
Your nails break against its wrapping paper.
Your wife tends the wounds you tell her nettles have caused.

Yet again my wet nurse wakes me from dreams of you.
Her fist clangs my door. Virginia died this way.
The weight of the stones carried her to her wet nurse.

What Orange Does

I have become obsessed with drawing houses for us
to live in. With each house I draw the hunger
for our happily ever after grows until it is a of my bed.

Your face blurs at times under the darkness but I know
it is still you whose arms I want to die in.
When I hear of your demise I watch from the back of the church

dressed in blue. It would have been easier for us
if we had been made from the same dirt.
We were both hungry for what the other had.

What Our Parents Don't Say About Orange:

The tunnel was dim. And I grew afraid
of the dark. You held my head to your chest,
the beat of your heart comforting me.

You are not Frida. Who said you were?
You are anything but her, for she is me and I am her.
Marry yourself then. You have married everyone else.

To clean yourself for her you have strung me up like a scarecrow.
Her curls are still intact. The ribs of my corset show hips
that will never bear young.

White

She tied a noose to hang me by, then made me hang myself.
The rope is too loose to choke me, too tight to let me go.
I hung there like a warning to others that would come after
me.

I traumatised a generation of Bolivian women,
so they never had daughters and never opened windows.
It was my fault watermelons never ripened in their hips.

My trip to the Americas is married with hate.
The two towers burn into my womb.
All I can do is watch.

What White Does:

I am growing old in your sweat.
The skin beneath my breasts creasing from your years
with her. I shall forget what it is to want.

The water is unforgiving, it drags you under its waves.
It will not let you play with it, the way a baby plays
in its tiny bath those first months.

With you I want to be brave enough to give up,
to be like that duckling swimming
in its first rain and just let go.

What Our Parents Don't Say About White:

Britain is my home, it built me the way Geppetto
built Pinocchio, limb by limb with pure love.
You took it all, then left without looking back.

It's the not knowing which makes me wake again
to love you. Let a corset of my bones wrap
round her like a fist. Then let her sing of love.

I am sorry. Sorry for the blankness.
Sometimes you have to turn all that love
to hate, just to survive.

ON LOSS

The man in the painting is not you. The face
is blurred. It is a face that could belong
to any man. Probably the artist didn't know
who he painted. This fact doesn't stop me
thinking you have sent me flowers,
when you haven't. I lunge into the block's
industrial bin and dig my body into waste
just to touch flowers that you might've
could've sent. But you have not
sent me flowers. Instead you sit at home,
cupped in your wife's body. This is what it is
to lose it all. To think one thing,
to think it so real that it becomes real
just for one moment. Then to see yourself
as your neighbours do; as a woman plunging into a bin.

GAËL
LE CORNEC

THE OTHER
Play Extract

The Other is a magic realist play about a refugee child running away from war.

In the previous scene we see the child, Mana and her inseparable doll companion Manita, bought in an auction by a Giant. Now Mana and Manita are trapped in the giant's hut. They are confined to the floor, on a corner of the hut. Manita is scared, so Mana tells her a bedtime story, a "girl" is the protagonist. Mana projects herself in both "the girl" and Manita and their stories reveal the truth of Mana's life in the giant's hut.

Characters:
Mana & Manita

Battered soil. Dried leaves,
Carcasses on the wall:
chickens, pigs, humans.

Don't worry, Manita, monsters will never catch a clever girl like you.
The moon is high, time to sleep
and dream of fairies.

Don't worry I said,
everything that's dark will go away

Alright, I'll tell you a story.
Ready?

In the beginning the nights
ran over the girl,
an old wheel on a parched road.

At dusk, the giant would come
to the girl's corner of the hut
and cut a lock
of her hair.

In the morning,
by magic,
her hair had grown back.
So night after night,
the giant returned, to cut
the same lock of hair

night after night, he'd take her
hair with him to his corner of the hut,
day after day,
by magic,

her hair returned even
more beautiful.
One night, the girl woke up
with the smell of blood.

It's okay, Manita,
It's not that bad.
Grandma told me girls carry all
the sadness of the world
and when they have no more
tears, their hearts bleed
down their legs.

They bleed their sadness out every month.

The girl stopped asking questions

She got used to the growing hair,
the monthly bleed, the silence.
Her chain was too short to reach the courtyard.
So she waited
until the giant fell asleep
to the sound of her hands cleaning.

Then, she would peek into the out there
through the only tiny window.

The dust kept falling from the sky,
for hours, nights, galaxies.

From the peephole window
the girl could see

blind men

blind walking, searching for a home
they no longer knew.
One of them got trapped in the storm
just outside the giant's hut.

He was only a boy,
a boy under the dust,
all night his cries
heard from the distance of feet,
steps and runs away.

(*dust falls*)

He was alone under the storm.

By dawn the girl could see his head
slowly replaced by pumpkin scales.
His tears had dried. His cries were gone.

The other pumpkin-headed soldiers
joined him bringing the smell of blood
and decaying dust.
Hundreds of them knives in hand,
walking under the storm.

Cutting everything they see,
cutting the trees,
the neighbouring huts,
cutting, cutting, cutting,
the giant's hut!

Cover yourself Manita, the dust!
don't let it touch you,
or you'll become one of them.

The girl grabbed the last leaf from the roof
and made herself as small as possible.
The soldiers sniff the air
blind searching
the giant joins them
they start walking towards the girl
giant men giant hands
approaching
the girl.

PATRIZIA LONGHITANO

I, THE POET.

One day I'll wake up and I'll be a real poet.
And I will tell you about the riding lamp, the futtock,
the glory hole and the monkey rail and you'll be laughing
while I'll reveal to you I was just talking about ships' parts.

Then, the night will come and I'll be whispering to you
things like British thermal unit, quantum bit
and centiliter and you'll be telling me your cold toes
are wriggling and to turn off the light.

On the morning of the second day, while you'll be still sleepy
I will explain to you the difference between the Talmud
and the Torah using only iambic pentameter
being careful to not overdo it with the alliterations.

At lunch, while I'll observe you cooking, I will let my lungs
and nostrils absorb the smell of the *porcini* you found
behind our weeping willow and I will write about the fried bread
and bananas I used to eat in Brazil when I was a child.

But on the third day, I'll be silent all morning
and just before our afternoon nap, I will notice
how you slightly bend your head when asking me something.

And while in bed waiting to fall asleep,
I will tell you that I saw the priest kissing the organist
and you will believe me because I will be a real poet.

TIME, THEY SAY IT'S RELATIVE

The year I was born, two young men died
in Sicily and their killers were never found.
I was two months old when they gave
each other their last kiss, their last embrace.

While I was surrounded by the Amazonian forest,
laughing and giggling to my mother,
maybe in that moment they were being pushed
in the car that brought them to that citrus grove.

When I was crying in the night,
my parents went to check me in my cot,
the two men were making love
imagining a future together.

From Giarra to Manaus there are
a little bit more than 9000km - between me
and those two bodies: between us a world
that we were supposed to discover and eat.

Giorgio and Toni. Giorgio, Toni and Patrizia.
Giorgio, Toni, Patrizia and the oceans, the deserts,
the hurricanes, the sharks, the metropolis, the meadows
and eagles and orchids in swamps and centuries-old trees…

My parents were imagining what I might
accomplish, who I might meet or love one day.
They were looking at the stars embracing each other
while the two boys got a bullet in their heads.

We were all breathing together.
We were all beings,
we were all being together…
and then not.

PRIGGISHNESS

Yes, I did hear it right or didn't I?
The two ladies at the bus stop
talking with their shopping bags
next to their swollen ankles.

Their clothes - a mix of lavender and talcum
their hands moving - a showing off of humongous rings
and then again, but this time clearer: '*Yes, I told you,*
she is not even second generation English.'

ARISTOTLE AND THE OCTOPUSES

On 6th April 2010, Parliament
Made slavery illegal in England.
Of course, my mother wasn't insane,
She was just a very sad and peculiar woman.
Only 58% of people really wash their hands
After visiting toilets and yes,
People do really go around and around
In circles when they are lost.
When I kissed a boy
For the first time, I realised
How everything made sense: saliva,
Muscles, electricity and noses.
If you want to weigh your head,
You need to put it in a bucket full of water
But if you want to weigh clouds
You need to use elephants.
So, is it true
That there is no petrol left in Sicily?
I asked my father yesterday.
There is nothing left in Sicily: it's pure chaos!
That's what he told me on Skype
While on Facebook I was chatting
With Frederick proud that probably
The next President in Finland will be gay.
But when I kissed a girl
For the first time, I realised
How everything is connected: guts,

Breaths, electricity and fingertips.
Not all oranges are orange
Most of them are just green
And octopuses don't have eight legs
But two: when they copulate,
The male inserts one of his arms,
Full of sperm, in the female's head.
I always found it ironic that the first American
Buried in Britain was Pocahontas.

LUIZA
SAUMA

AGNES AGNES AGNES

1.

A DOZEN OF us were crowded round a table at a pub in Camden. All girls. It was my sixteenth birthday. We never had a problem getting served, though our favourite drinks should have given us away: Bacardi Breezers, vodka and orange, snakebite and black. We all thought Nirali was the classy one, because she drank gin and tonic.

Georgia arrived late. She brought a friend – someone I had never met before, who looked neither like a girl nor a boy. The stranger had short blond hair and hazel eyes so pale they almost seemed yellow.

'Who's that weird boy?' said Nirali, leaning in close. Her long black hair tickled my bare shoulder.

'I'm not sure it's a boy.'

'You're joking, right?'

Georgia saw us and came over, with the boy-girl close behind.

'Happy birthday!' she said, as we hugged. 'This is my friend Agnes. Agnes, meet Juliana.'

Agnes smiled and bowed. She might even have kissed my hand, like a Victorian gent, but I can't remember. I might have made that up. Mostly, I remember how beautiful she looked, but not like a girl – like a choir boy or a teen idol. River Phoenix, but with softer features. Just as handsome.

'Happy birthday,' she said. 'Hope you don't mind me gatecrashing your party.'

'It's not really a party.'

Agnes put her hands into the pockets of her studded leather jacket and hung back as Georgia and I caught up on things. How her relationship with her boyfriend was going. They hadn't had sex but were in talks about it. Only a handful of girls in our year had done it, and they were all weird: theatre geeks or townies, but not real townies. You couldn't be a townie when you went to a fancy girls' school like ours.

'So you're gonna do it?' I said.

'I think so,' said Georgia, half-smiling, half-grimacing.

'You should do it.'

'Really?'

'Why not?'

'You haven't done it either.'

'You should do it first,' I said. 'Tell me what it's like.'

Agnes leaned in and said, 'Do you fancy a drink?'

Georgia flicked her blond hair, held up her vodka and orange, and said, 'I'm all right.'

'Juliana, you want one?'

'Are you sure?'

'Yeah.'

'Can I have a watermelon Bacardi Breezer?'

Agnes grinned toothily and went off to the bar. A few minutes later she brought back my drink – a bright pink alcopop – and a pint of beer for herself.

'How can you drink that stuff?' I said.

'It grows on you. Go on, try it.'

I took a sip of her pint and almost missed my mouth, so that it splashed on my T-shirt.

'Urgh. No. That's an old-man drink.'

Agnes laughed in that enunciated way of hers. Ha ha ha. She insisted on buying all my drinks for the rest of the night, until I was completely wasted. Like every other weekend, my friends and I drank until we were sick on Camden High Street. This time, Agnes was the one who held back my hair.

'Your hair,' she said, as I stood up straight. 'It's beautiful.'

'Is it?'

'Like dark honey.'

I brushed it back with my hands and tried to focus on her face.

2.

Her name was Agnes St John and her father was a Tory grandee. An old guy, as white as paper, who I had seen on TV when my parents watched the news. I made fun of her for that, the night we met, because my parents were radical Brazilian academics who had campaigned against the military dictatorship and exiled themselves to London, where I was born. She was in the last year of sixth form and lived off Kensington High Street in a tall white house, with weekends on the Norfolk coast. I was doing my GCSEs, lived in Hendon and went to private school on a scholarship, though my grades had slipped. Grades didn't matter to Agnes. She knew people.

3.

Agnes called me the day after my birthday to ask me if I was feeling OK. I didn't get hangovers back then. I could drink and drink and drink and wake up feeling fine. When I told her so, over the phone, she laughed and told me to stop bragging. Then she asked me to meet her at Piccadilly Circus tube station.

When I arrived she was leaning against a wall, wearing the same blue jeans and black leather jacket she had been wearing the night before, one foot lifted against the wall. I was wearing the same black make-up, blurred over my eyelids.

She saw me, nodded boyishly, and said, 'Are you hungry?'

'I could eat a horse.'

'I've made a reservation.'

'A reservation?'

'It's a surprise.'

We walked out of the station, towards Soho. It was a warm spring day. Her leather-jacketed arm held firmly onto mine, making me feel light-headed. She was looking straight ahead, a delighted smile on her face.

'Where are you taking me?'

She turned and winked. When we arrived at Sherwood Street, she stopped walking.

'Here we are.'

We were at L'Abattoir, a restaurant housed in a tall Art Deco building, its stained glass windows twinkling in the sun. I was vaguely aware that it was a celebrity hangout, and very expensive indeed.

'You're joking.'

'Have you eaten here before?'

'No, have you?'

'It's pretty good.'

She took my arm again and led me inside. It was a huge, cavernous place – more like a nightclub than a restaurant. Waiters in black and white walked about with graceful haste. Glasses clinked. Cutlery scratched on china. I hated that sound – I still do – and a shiver ran down my spine. A maitre d' approached. Even though we looked odd in those surroundings – two casually dressed teenage girls – there wasn't a flicker of doubt on his face. He was a pro. Or maybe he recognised her.

'We have a reservation,' said Agnes. 'Under St John.'

'Right this way.'

As soon as we sat down she told me that that her father had a tab, so we could eat anything we wanted.

'Are you sure?' I said, with my eye on the lobster.

She smiled, knowing that I was impressed. I watched her skimming the menu with those yellow-hazel eyes, trying to imagine her as the girl her parents intended her to be. A débutante. Long blond hair, lipstick and mascara, a silk blouse with a pussy-bow. I could almost see it. She would have been a beautiful girl.

A waiter brought a bottle of champagne and popped it in front of us, making all the other diners look at us with curiosity. We giggled like the schoolgirls we were, and he poured it into our glasses, careful that it didn't fizz over.

'I didn't hear you order champagne,' I whispered.

'You can't have oysters without champagne.'

'You're so posh.'

'So are you.'

'No. You're *really* posh.'

I took a sip of champagne and closed my eyes as it bubbled in my mouth. When I opened them, Agnes was leaning back in her chair, staring at me.

'You're looking at me funny,' I said.

'You're gorgeous.'

'Shut up! I'm not.'

'You are.'

'Is this a date?'

'Would you like it to be?'

'I've never been on a date before.'

'Not even with a boy?'

'No, but I've kissed a few.' I drank more champagne. 'Boys never act the way I want them to.'

'Maybe you're meeting the wrong boys.'

'Or maybe I'm gay.'

'You're not,' she said.

The oysters came and we swallowed them down, with vinaigrette dribbling down our chins. Then the lobster and a bottle of Sauvignon Blanc, which Agnes chose as though she had some knowledge of wine.

She asked me about my family, about Brazil. I told her that I was an only child, that I didn't speak Portuguese, but I could vaguely understand my parents when they spoke to each other. When we visited Brazil, though, people talked faster and I couldn't keep up. Most of my relatives spoke to me in broken English – apart from my grandparents, with whom I could barely communicate.

'It would be nice to have an excuse not to speak to my family,' said Agnes.

'It makes me feel like an outsider.'

'That's the best way to feel.'

Some outsider, I thought, with a tab at L'Abattoir. But I didn't say that.

I asked her about her life, but she was hazy on the details. She didn't want to talk about her famous father, who was in his eighties and had been in the news recently, attacking the new Labour government. Nor her mother, who was several decades younger and sometimes appeared in *Tatler*.

'Do you have siblings?' I said.

'I have two half-brothers. They're really old.'

She didn't say more than that.

4.

Before we met, Agnes had been collecting wives. She told me all about it. Every holiday she took with her family she would end up fucking some married woman in a villa or chalet. Fucking, I thought. Is that the right word? It didn't turn me on, the thought of Agnes having sex with middle-aged housewives. The rolls of flesh. The wrinkles. I tried not to think about it. Instead, I wondered whether she wore a swimming costume by the pool. I couldn't imagine it. I could only imagine her in a pair of swimming trunks, with a chest as flat as a boy's.

'But now I have you,' she said, as we lay on her bed, smoking weed.

She threw the roach out of the window and wrapped her legs and arms around me. I stiffened and then wrapped myself around her, too, because that's what she wanted. I could feel her heart beating against my chest. Agnes Agnes Agnes. When I shifted, I felt a small, soft breast pressing against me. She wasn't flat-chested; she wasn't a boy. If I didn't move, I couldn't feel it. I lay very still.

5.

I was smoking cigarettes with Nirali and Georgia at the far end of the lacrosse field when two girls from year ten crawled out of the bushes. They giggled and walked up to us, brushing leaves from their tartan skirts.

'Got a cigarette?' said the tall, skinny one. She had short hair and walked with an easy swagger.

'Here,' I said, handing one over with a lighter.

She lit it and passed it to her friend, who was smaller and more curvaceous. We were all rubbing our hands together to keep warm, even though it was spring.

'What were you doing in the bushes?' said Nirali.

'Just had sex,' said the short girl.

'Gross,' said Georgia, and we all burst out laughing. 'Juliana's a lesbian too.'

'Shut up, Georgia.'

'She's got a posh girlfriend from Kensington who wines and dines her,' said Nirali, cackling.

'And you've never even pulled anyone,' I said, 'so shut up.'

'Oh, that's nice.' Nirali lit another cigarette, looking pissed off.

'Who's your girlfriend?' said the tall girl.

'Can we talk about something else?'

'Agnes St John,' said Nirali.

'You're going out with Agnes St John?' said the short girl, her eyes wide and bright.

'You know her?'

'Everyone knows Agnes.'

6.

Over the summer, Agnes and I spent two weeks in Paris. I told my parents that her family was going with us, but they weren't.

Agnes paid for our Eurostar tickets, our meals, everything. We stayed on a sofa-bed in Le Marais, in a flat rented by her friends James and Suzanne, who were twins. They were nineteen and would seem like children to me now, but at the time, they were so sophisticated that I could barely speak in their presence. Nothing had to be explained about Agnes and me. As soon as we walked through the door, she said, 'This is my girlfriend, Juliana' and they barely reacted.

'She's Brazilian,' said Agnes.

'That's cool,' said Suzanne, lying supine on the floor.

They had people round most nights to drink wine, smoke spliffs and talk about the books and screenplays they wanted to write, while I sat on the corner of the sofa, holding my glass and saying nothing, trying to be cool. My mother destroyed my ruse by calling the flat nearly every day. The twins or their friends would hand over the phone, smirking.

'Who are these people who answer the phone?' my mother once said.

'Agnes's cousins.'

'They always sound stoned. Are *you* stoned?'

'Mum, stop it!'

Nothing was more embarrassing than having parents who loved you.

I walked the streets of Paris with Agnes on my arm, pretending to be free, like James and Suzanne. But I was totting up in my head all the work I had to do when we returned to London. My A-levels would be starting soon. I had my heart set on Cambridge, because it would make my immigrant parents proud.

I loved feeling the cool summer air on my bare legs, going to galleries, eating steak frites, pretending to be grown-ups. We bought a padlock from a man on the Pont des Arts, wrote our names on it, locked it on the wire fence and threw the key into the Seine. Agnes pulled me towards her and gave me a soft kiss. I didn't care who saw us. Not only because it made me feel like a rebel, but because I knew that most passersby would be thinking, what a beautiful, beautiful boy.

7.

One night Agnes went out with Suzanne to buy cigarettes and I was left alone with James. We were pretty drunk – it was nearly midnight. He was racking lines of cocaine onto the coffee table. I was both horrified and thrilled. I had never seen coke before, let alone taken it.

'You want some?' His blue eyes glimmered in the dim light, and creased when he smiled, like an adult.

'OK.'

'Have you done it before?'

'Uh, yeah, of course.'

He giggled, like he didn't believe me, and handed me a rolled banknote. I knew what to do; I'd seen it in films. He held my hair back as I snorted a line and then I sat back, tasting bitterness at the back of my throat, feeling a sort of jittery joy. He did a line and leaned back, with his arm casually around me.

'You know, you don't seem like a dyke.'

'I'm not a dyke.'

His face was inches away from mine. I could feel his breath on my mouth, the sweet tang of red wine.

'So how come you're with Agnes?'

We heard a key in the lock and James sprung upwards, onto his feet. Agnes and Suzanne walked into the flat, laughing about something or other.

'Hey!' said James. 'You took your time.'

'We ran into some people,' said Suzanne. 'They're all going to a party. Do you guys wanna go?'

'OK, yeah.'

Agnes came over and sat where James had been sitting. I wondered if she could feel the warmth from his body on the sofa. She kissed me on the lips and smiled.

8.

Agnes and I were sitting on the sofa-bed. We hadn't folded it away yet. Everyone else was out. We did many things on that bed – kiss, sleep, eat, smoke, drink, watch French television; everything short of taking our clothes off. We were smoking out of the window, listening to a Robert Johnson CD and talking about how much we would miss seeing each other every day, once I was back at school. Agnes had got mediocre A-levels and didn't know what she was doing next. It didn't seem to trouble her.

There was a pause in the conversation before she said, 'We've never had sex.'

'No.' I avoided her eyes.

'Why?'

I felt my face go red. I stuck it further out of the window, partly to feel the breeze and partly to hide my embarrassment. There were dozens of people walking up and down the street, pushing prams, tugging along dogs, holding briefcases.

'I'm not going to pressure you into anything. I was just wondering why we never talk about it.'

'Even my straight friends don't have sex.'

'What about Georgia?'

Indeed, since losing her virginity, Georgia had slept with five different boys – one of whom was actually a man, our former English teacher Mr Gregory. Tom, she called him. He didn't work at our school any more, so it was all perfectly legal.

'Georgia doesn't count. She's a total slut.'

'Ha!'

'I don't feel ready for it. You're acting like a boy.'

'Isn't that why you go out with me, Juli?'

'No.'

I could feel that my face had returned to its normal colour, so I looked up at her and threw my cigarette out the window.

'I go out with you because I love you,' I said.

I pulled her towards me – which felt funny, because usually she was the one who pulled me towards her – and kissed her on the lips. She stroked my breasts, which was allowed, and then I touched hers, which I didn't usually allow, but which felt all right. I could feel a tingle passing from her lips onto mine, curving down my spine, down and down.

'OK. I'll do it.'

9.

The next day, we returned to London. On the train, we held hands under the table as we talked about Paris, school, James and Suzanne, but I was counting down the minutes until we reached Waterloo. It was like a light being switched off.

Agnes called me the next day, but I didn't answer, and I didn't answer the day after or the day after that. I went back to school, back to the teachers telling me that I wouldn't get into Cambridge in my wildest dreams. I knew they were wrong, those old hags.

I didn't open the letters that came for me every other day, making my mother suspicious. She thought we were just friends – very good friends. I had never brought Agnes over, because I knew that Mum would know it, as soon as she saw her.

'Why so many letters?' she said. 'It's like you're obsessed with each other.'

'Maybe she's obsessed with me. I'm not obsessed with her.'

I burned the letters in a metal bin in our garden. When I came back inside, my father was reading the paper over a cup of coffee.

'Casting spells?' he said.

'Cale boca.'

'It's *cala* boca.'

'Oh just shut up!'

This carried on for several weeks. I started rejecting the calls as soon as I saw her name flash up. And then they stopped.

10.

The night I celebrated my A-level results, I got a phone call at 4 am. I was on a night-bus to Hendon, with my boyfriend sitting next to me. I must have been half-asleep when it rang, giving me a jolt. A number I didn't recognise.

'Hello?'

No answer.

'Hello?'

No answer.

'Who is this? I'm going to hang up.'

I heard a breath. I knew that breath.

'I just wanted to say well done,' she said.

And then she hung up.

'Who was that?' said Simon.

'Wrong number.'

11.

Last week I was walking in Soho on a lovely spring evening, one of those that lifts you from your winter fug, making you think, Ah, life isn't so bad. I was going to meet Nirali, who I hadn't seen in months, at a restaurant just a few streets away from where L'Abattoir used to be. The building is still there, but L'Abattoir closed down a long time ago. It's now an enormous coffee shop.

Everything was going pale blue in the twilight, with the sun just peeping over the buildings. I heard a familiar laugh – bright and boyish – and my guts felt like they had turned inside out. I turned and caught a glimpse of a good-looking man in his thirties, dressed expensively dapper. Pinstripe suit, polished brogues, shining blond hair cut into a crop. He was walking down the street arm-in-arm with a young woman in a red dress and heels. They walked right past me without a glance. I turned towards the window of a newsagent, pretending to read a poster.

'Where are you taking me?' said the woman, with laughter in her voice. Her heels clicked on the pavement.

'It's a surprise.'

I easily caught up with them and then managed to get ahead, so that I was walking ten metres in front. I turned and looked at them, head-on. He wasn't a man. Or was he? Her face was thinner, sharper – moulded into a different, adult shape – but I knew it was her. Agnes. She didn't look at me. Not even a glance. Maybe she didn't see me. I was wearing my work suit. A couple of stones heavier. Fifteen years older. Unrecognisable, perhaps.

I started walking in the opposite direction, further into Soho, to meet Nirali. I was late. I decided I wouldn't tell her about Agnes. What could I say?

'I saw the ghost of Agnes St John, walking on Brewer Street.'

12.

'Are you sure?'

'Yes.'

'You're sure that you're sure?'

'Stop asking. Otherwise I'll change my mind. Then you'll be sorry.'

Her eyes went small and she laughed. Ha ha ha. I sat up and pulled my T-shirt off. Then I stood up, took off my jeans, bra and knickers, walked to the stereo and turned it up – Robert Johnson's 'Walkin' Blues'. I could hear birds singing and traffic humming on Rue Saint-Gilles and clothes being dropped onto the floor. Could feel the breeze from the open window, brushing against my body, making the hairs on my thighs stand on end. Agnes behind me, waiting.

JUANA ADCOCK

THE CHRISTMAS TREE

A couple of months ago I had my skin surgically removed and replaced with a network of incandescent light bulbs in four different colours, like a Christmas tree. Each time I breathe in, the lights swell and expand a little, blurring at the edges as if trying to cover the gaps in between. When I breathe out, it's like I'm blowing out a candle, and for a moment I am still in my own darkness. Then I'm on again.

/ Off. // On. /// Off. /// On. // / Off. // On. // ///

My favourite thing is to try and make my lights reach further and further, just to see how far I can go. So I might be sitting in this little room but my skin reaches all the way to Brazil sometimes. It's a strange feeling, my muscles and bones and things all exposed, tingly and warm from the light bulbs. I can't quite tell if it hurts or feels good. The breeze is slightly astringent on my organs. I don't like to look down, though. I'm afraid I might make myself feel sick seeing myself open up like that. Or I might be too tempted to pry the gaps wider and contemplate the inner workings of my body. No. What I want to do is send colourful, intermittent lights as far as they will reach. Did you know that the favelas in Brazil are already painted in bright colours? I'd seen them in pictures before but they really are bright beyond description. So taking my Christmas lights there might seem like carrying river stones to the river. But still, that's what I do.

THE SERPENT DIALOGUES (an extract)

5

But the snake also had violent mood swings, and the woman suffered immensely for it. Some days he gave her the most fascinating answers, other days he was silent, or sarcastic.[1] That's when the woman started to doubt her own sanity, wondering whether she was the one who was in his space,[2] the balcony not being hers but his, with him being gracious enough to allow her to visit. But even when the snake was in the foulest mood, the woman never wanted to sever the connection, because she felt their dialogues always taught her something.

---

1 Let go, foot of snow
melt in hand, melt in sun

2 A fundamental error of attribution
eggs most fiction on:
to say "mine", "his", "hers"
to call ourselves the owners
as we walk through the forest
along trails built by the tread of wolves

In this respect, the woman was a formalist.[3]

W: Snake, what's the true nature of desire?

S: Everyone asks me that. Don't you have anything more interesting to talk about? That's like asking the moon about the mysteries of love

W: OK, what's your opinion on Rumi's poem about the mouse and the frog?

S: Is that something like the little mermaid? I can't stand stories about princesses

---

3 O heartbreak, old friend!
We preferred to live off the fault lines,
where the pressure builds and rock is lifted.
In the shoogling of things
in our hermit huts
in a place of tension
never resting!
I wanted to tell you how much
our conversations shook up my mind,
set me forth from my stasis
into a planetary motion.
But already I could feel you touch the valley of my neck
and wrap your fingers around.
As you gently squeezed, I could see you flirt
with the idea of strangulation.
Already feeling the glottis
close in your grip
I implored, "Let's live together in a tiny room
and drive each other crazy. It's what lovers
do!"

W: Human induced climate change and mass extinction of the species. You must have strong opinions on that

S: Terrible. What else?

W: What do you do when you can't sleep?

S: I don't sleep. What else?

6

Then one day the snake didn't show up at all. Her mind scrambled for an explanation for what had happened, whether she'd said or done something offensive, whether she'd misunderstood. She called out from her balcony all day long: Snake! Snake!

It occurred to her it might be some sort of demonstration on his part, a lesson on the structure of desire itself. She cut out a rectangle in the middle of a blank page. She gazed into that window: *look at where desire lives,* she told herself. She made lists of things the snake might be trying to teach her about desire:

1) to create desire you must play with expectation: create a pattern, then break it
2) desire is a friendly embrace that suddenly turns electric
3) desire draws a rosette that starts at the chest and then dances around the whole body
4) desire is also the impulse to run away from what we've done

She thought absence was the snake's method, and she paid attention like a loyal disciple. She began waiting at the balcony two hours earlier than the usual time, observing desire as it swerved around inside her flesh: a rabid monkey thrashing against metal bars. She took note of the shapes, colours, tastes of its rage. She kept a journal, to analyse all its components:

Day 19

The sky continues to grumble like a hungry belly.

Day 21

The phone vibrates and I obey
rising from my chair where I am nestled with a book
I listen as the sun
draws a rib bone across the sky

I remember an artist who operated on himself
cut open his own chest,
carved out a rib bone,
sewed himself back up,
offered the bone to his mother
as a necklace,
and she, half guiltily, half glad,
obliged. What art
can ever be made after this?

Day 22

To befriend my boredom, my wanting.
To notice how it takes hold of me.
How, when I decided otherwise,
and went on a long walk
wearing sandals, despite threats of rain,
I paid attention to this pulse, to the way
the plants shook
and quivered in the wind, as if in perpetual
longing. This longing
also a part
of –

And then
words, mixing lust and *tenerezza*,
appear unexpected on my screen.

The sky roars, annoyed
at my distractedness.

It seems all I care about is
this impossible encounter, an instant
through the bits and bytes,
up to the stratosphere, through a satellite
then back to earth again:

✓✓ *seen 22:03*

Am I really –

All we've

ever
really
wanted
is
to be seen.

To be scene:
watched, contemplated
accepted

Day 23

In the big room, in the church, the place I was so afraid of at night.
I finally come here to work.
To be without internet, to get right down to it.

And I discover the mirror I have been without all these days. The mirror I never wanted to see myself in. That in the dark I was so afraid of.

Switching on the light, those two seconds of terror before the tungsten blinks.
The terrible silence of knick knacks, flung
the broken musical instruments
their tune like the skeleton
of a mouse in formol

And I watch as
my brain turns to my phone: wanting wanting wanting

to be

Day 24

In my body, full of scrolling. Scrolls of the dead sea, always down, down, not reaching. Always eating but never nourished. Mistaking this hunger for a particular need, rather than a dis-ease. Before television, we used to sit round the fire and perform for each other.

We still do, but in a way that makes us feel utterly alone—our faces lit by the ice blue of the fire-screen.

I Google this, and the internet says that what I'm feeling is completely normal, that there are hundreds of thousands of people like me, scattered around the globe. We tell each other our most dreadful secrets, this is our way to be home. My fingers like crabs, moving sideways on the keyboard. I wanted always to be by your side. It didn't matter to me that you were a miser, dry kindling, half of your body crushed by heartbreak, and that you no longer believed in life. I wanted to hook onto your arm and walk through the streets, heels clapping against cobblestone, and feel protected.

To instead be one's own wife –

Day 25

I post a selfie

take myself sweetly

to the stage
or the altar

bring myself flowers
and rain

Day 26

I reach for my phone
to check the time
when I can't remember the word
to be entertained
when something hurts, to see what it means
when I can't remember the way
when I know the way but want to make sure
when I don't know the train times
when I know the train times but want to make sure
when the sun is setting, igniting a bridge in the sky
to document this moment
to experience this moment
to experience myself documenting this moment
to document myself experiencing myself documenting
a moment I'm experiencing
when I'm lonely, to see what others are doing
when I'm uninformed, to see what others are broadcasting
when I can't remember the lyrics, or the tune, to this song
to do my shopping, while at the gym
to open my yoga app, while at work
to arrange a date, while on the toilet
to read an article, while walking from A to B
to check my email, while in the queue at the post office
to see, just to see, if anyone remembered me today

to be annoyed, if someone insists on an earlier message
I forgot to respond to

my phone to fill in all the gaps

Day 27

To paraphrase the cheesy Charlie Chaplin meme
I saw in a picture-frame on the pizzeria wall today:
silence is gold; we tend to buy noise instead.

And something about reaching for my phone as a form of
noise or interference, like wanting
to be saved from experiencing this instant
with all its beautiful and devastating aloneness

Day 28

The internet tells me that
Hiraeth is Welsh for
"homesickness for a home that you cannot
return to, or that never was"

I am split between this word and its exact opposite:
"a feeling of being at home in the unknown
in which you always are,
and which has always been"

TRUTH IS STRUCTURED LIKE A FICTION

Truth is structured like a fiction:
As if to teach me una lección, como si tomara
disciplinary action, the microphone fell
on my keyboard, breaking off
the accent key, chingándose
la tecla del acento, como para decirme:

Thou shalt renounce your own language.

MAIA
ELSNER

ON NOT-TRANSLATING NERUDA

Es verdad que el ámbar contiene / las lágrimas de las sirenas? (Pablo Neruda)
Is it true that amber contains / the tears of mermaids? (translation by William O'Daly)
Is it true that amber holds / the tears of mermaids? (my translation)

before translation
the reflexive speaks
a certain intimacy,
palms pressed, a child
finding her own
fingertips, an infinity
in decimal spaces skimmed
between nought and one
refracting shadows, each
held, diminished thing
a sunset stumbled on
the years inside

tomorrow
when *es verdad* is both
a question &
a statement. The Taxonomer
translates *contiene* as
contains. Then
caught up, he overlooks
a figure passing, gloves
clasped
clutching
identity
its fragility,
in a glance that tears itself
in translation
now hard now cold. But
in Spanish, *con* signifies *with,* as in
contigo en una noche estrellada
contigo hasta la luz del día se suicida
bajo una ola morada
enamorada, the tears of mermaids

he misses
the difference
between *contains* and *holds*–
will he contain his lover
will he hold his lover's tears
will he grasp closeness
in another language
when Anglo-Saxon gives
the only word for *love* he'll ever know
instead he'll choose a shoebox
emptied, used
for balls of string, he does not hear
beyond interpretation
two voices melted yellow &
a mayfly's lifespan
twenty-four hours
preserved
in gossamer wings

I. Lion Seal from the Assyrian Empire

in profile   etherized   on the cabinet
under glass   in green gypsum,   carved
from Uruk   a lion head   in bas-relief,
traces of   incising   you can’t quite see
all its scratchings &   in reverse   only when printed
an antelope   emerges   on cheap clay. It is
only in   the replicable object   that
the image is seen–   predator   presseddown
exposing its   hunted prey, consumed   quintessence, so
sealed   up in potential,   precious this stone
markings   hardly visible until revealed   in print, just a mimicry

II. Huipil from the Mayan Empire

Pulling vermillion   seedcrushed through a loom   agave-fibre dyed
a purple deep   this originates   from sea snails, then
the Conquest brings wool   establishes   a trade-route
from Cadiz   to Veracruz   overland
to Acapulco, then to China   silkwoven   in Arab blue
pattern tells   the Fall   of Cordoba
of 1492   in cross-stitch–the tree   of life
replaced by   crucifix, Mesquita geometry   reused for
a Cathedral. From Yaxchilan   in limestone   the Empress carved is wearing
in 709AD   a huipil   more than one thousand years of
identity   memory   history wiped out
encased   as stacks of goods   shipped across ocean
edges   cut up countries   leaving blank space
all left out to dry   all torn   all stitched together

V. Dislocated Figure, Period Unknown

Chicana girl   in gender neutral clothes   stares out fixed notions
hangs out   with pachuca,   both
performing   identity: they are   inscribed as artists, each appropriates
another's face, becomes   *Las Tres Marias*   suddenly
now   Guadalupe   Malinche
Llorona   in   distinguishable
in the Texan sun   replica   as whore, then
mother-   virgin   assimilated
losing her children   to foreign soil, now   made into typecast
on street corners   hemmed in   as immigrant
or   as second generation   always immigrant
racialised   as one who loses   and that same story–
woman anchoring babies   spins a yarn, so   begins another prayer
on both knees   *virgencita*   *that Carlitos*
find a job   *virgencita*   *help Anita*
get well   *virgencita*   *forgive me what I said*
between whispers   conch shell & incense smoke   Tonantzin breathes

POLISH HONEY CAKE

i.

We inherit the ritual. Orange skins peeled,
we try to boil away

the bitterness, the way
my grandmother boils

hot milk, the way it overflows, the way
there's not enough

milk, and too much
skin

ii.

My grandmother takes pills.
My grandmother makes me eat

each grain of rice. There is no room
for leftovers. My father says

this comes from trauma. That rice is never simply
rice. You add sugar to the boiling, this boils out

bitterness, this assimilates, softens
all kinds of things

iii.

I learn to distill water. I learn to kill
bacteria. I learn

to eat my rice. Taken hot, the water
scalds, each blistered throat

is one less scream

iv.

My grandmother opts for silence.
The thing she's not got over –

what it is to live. Is this the purpose
of all those stories of survival. To make heroes

of us. To convince ourselves that living
is not some kind

of violence. Is there a reason for
indifference

v.

These things I know:
you panic in front of the police.

When they search for explosives.
When there are no explosives.

After sugar, stir in raisins
and sultanas. There is an order.

Each year we replicate
the order. I must eat

each grain of rice

TRANSNATIONAL ZOO

BOARD OF TRUSTEES

Enclosure Act, 1773. Carves up hills. Little boxes made of ticky-tacky to put sheep in. Then, discussion in Parliament over dry stone walls. Then, worry that a fox might slink in, might bring offspring, might invade rabbit-hutches, denigrate chicken coops, might steal sheep. One politician cries wolf. The rest abnegate responsibility. They call this consensus. In 1939, the Spanish resistance are abandoned. Some make it through Madrid. Some fall in Barcelona, and a red sun falls over Sète. One evening, a bedraggled troop boards a ship. On the deck, a red-legged partridge alights. Cocks its head, furls its wings, and is gone.

MAMMAL

She is borrowed by coyotes. She lends her nape, her back, her spine, for toughening. She lengthens into a hide, thickening, mirrors the dusk. In the day, she soaks dishrags at the watering hole, stitches each together with cochineal thread, this fishing rod, dips in, and disappears. Then the dye washes out, detaching itself into petalsnewly fallen, from the bougainvillea up above. What remains, she sells at street corners. Sometimes, she invents to pass the time. Another context. Another name. Sometimes, she wonders, in what language rain falls on tormented cities. Soon, the figs ripen.

PREY

He fell to the wrath of Artemis. She, to the corner at *Calzada de Tlalpan*. There was a sacrifice that day. On the shore, are washerwomen. They clean the Big House, on tourist visas, renewed each day. To the border, he tracks them, the sea slipping over stones. They say the moon lost her virginity, that night, and the sun shred itself against the rocks. She was dragged. Dragged through Juarez & Zapata, by General Anaya, spread out, finally, at his foot. By Francisco Sosa, she was gutted, her antlers removed, her hide skinned, while he was torn by hairless dogs in Coyoacan square.

ZOO KEEPER

In old manuscripts, small difference there is between *s* and *f*. Take Cotton Nero, for instance, Gawain wandering, a pearl glinting, poised at the brink. And the river rising, the swell-surge into flood. Then, new translations, new transliterations encode distinction. The banks of the Mississippi are hemmed in. Now, a catfish thrusts through jet-quartz. Quicksilver ripples over skin. Its membrane, permeable. A great, rusted hook clenching in. Then, a Council of Elders in Illinois. They reverse the Chicago, this great feat of foreign intervention, now flushing sewage to the gulf of Mexico, massaging children as they swim. Deposited on the shore: oil-spill rainbows, bits of shell.

CAGE

In the Bible, Adam gave each animal its name. Kan. Chakmool. Chuwen. Chapulin. Aak. Aayin. Lexu. Quetzal. When the Summer Institute got their hands on it, there'd already been a fall, and few words left, uncorrupted. In the Lacandona forest, you hear them still, while Akyantho', god of foreigners, brings his pistol & light skin, & Jesus Christ, his son, hangs out with Tuub & Kisin. Some names remain. Some are lost in (mis)translation, as preacher and zoologist transcribe secrets, sell-off selves. Then the rain came, and others washed away. Now, the Authorities turn people into birds. Some nests are burned. Some wings are broken.

ARMANDO CELAYO

FEARLESS FREAK

(an extract from Downward Is Heavenward)

Everyone knew him for his movies, these hour-long films about folks he called fearless freaks. The minorities in the minorities. "It's one thing being an outcast," Milo, my brother, once explained in an interview, after he'd received an honorable mention from a film institute out west. "But an outcast among the outcasts—man, that's something else."

It was his third short, *Mudo*, that earned him acclaim from critics. *Mudo*'s about this Chicano kid. Mudo avoids the world by hiding behind the long drapes of his dark hair, and he's always listening to his WalkMan, usually blasting some early Flaming Lips: *Hit To Death In The Future Head, In A Priest Driven Ambulance*—that kind of stuff. Mudo's got this slow-eyed look, like he's been huffing spray paint from a Coke can. He doesn't say a thing throughout the movie, but you know what he's thinking—what he's feeling, really—when he starts sketching in his scrawled-on notebook and the black-and-white screen lights up with his drawings. Words—snippets of dialogue from when he's getting bitched-out by his dad, or when he overhears a conversation from the girl he's crushing on—morph into this little cartoon creature. Part Mickey Mouse and part Swamp Thing, it's supposed to represent Mudo's voice, the emotion he can't articulate. At least, that's how Milo once broke it down for me, years and years after he made *Mudo*, when he fell back home to us, his skinny body as frail as birdbones. Every time I watch the movie now, his explanation makes sense. When Mudo's sitting in the school cafeteria, glancing at his crush a few tables away, and the Creature appears next to her, invisible to everyone but Mudo. It reaches out its scabby hand, hoping to strum her fluffy red hair, but slowly pulls back, crestfallen—that's yearning turning into resignation. Self-hate: Mudo's sitting on his disheveled bed and carving puffy red marks into his forearm—his dad's outside, shouting all kinds of shit, and shoulder-slamming himself into the barricaded door—while the Creature's curled into a scrunched-up question mark on the floor, broken musical notes hovering as a halo around his head.

One critic described the movie dead-on: "*Slacker* meets *Fantasia* for Chicanos."

*

Unsurprisingly, *Mudo* was autobiographical. Wearing flannel shirts and steeltoed boots he bought from the Salvation Army, he showed up at Capitol Hill, a high school fifty-fiftied between black and Latino kids, Milo didn't score himself any points from the Dickies-sporting cholos by kicking it with the stragglers of white stoners. "Puto sellout," los vatos locos would hiss at him, tripping him as he tried to sneak by them in the hallway. "Greasy wetbacks," Milo murmured as soon as they were out of earshot.

But Milo's crowd had nothing to do with selling out or identity politics; back then he didn't care about that stuff. "Why do we hang out with the people we hang out with?" he once said in a zine. "Music."

While all the other kids at Capitol Hill were split listening either to Garth Brooks or Bon Jovi or Color Me Badd, Milo and his friends were proud patch-wearing members of the Sub Pop Singles Club. I still have most of those old tapes, stuffed away in one of my boxes of Milo's ephemera, along with dozens of interviews I tracked down through libraries and the internet, and piles of the holey clothes he wore everyday, and his first camera—stolen, of course—along with the crumbling reels of his earliest footage—artifacts collected and arranged to piece together a patchwork portrait of my brother as a young artist, a half-made mosaic of who he was and wasn't.

Milo stuck out from his clique in one important way. Though they all liked to skip classes to get high, Milo would get blazed with his boys then bury his head in his art. Baroque pencil-and-ink sketches of his friends passed out on the couch, every white space on the wide-ruled page drawn and drawn upon. As soon as he figured out how to break into the supplies closet at school and how to discreetly pocket brushes from Home Depot, Milo started painting. All his friends' faces looked like they were made of bark and mud.

By his senior year, Milo got serious about metalwork.

Our father, Camilo, worked the welding line at Oklahoma Steel and Wire, mainly soldering train axles as big as a VW Bug. Monday through Thursday, he'd clock-in by six in the morning at the latest and would get home just as Mom and I were setting up the table for dinner. While we ate, no one spoke except for Camilo, who always bitched about his pendejo coworkers at the factory—rants that were normally racist against white and black people and his fellow Mexican immigrants. "They should let me run the place," he'd say to end his tirades, "then some real work would get done." Afterwards, when Mom and I finished clearing the leftovers and washing the dishes, the two of us went to her bedroom to catch up on our soaps: *Guiding Light* and *Knots Landing*. I'd rest my head on her lap as she stroked my hair, faintly humming some tune I assumed was from her childhood, and soon I drifted off. Across the hall, Milo shut himself away in his room, a soft pulse of music rumbling through his postered door. On his own, Camilo slouched in front of the living room TV, watching the Rangers lose another ballgame while slow-sipping from a mug of orange juice and tequila until he fell asleep in his recliner. His snores would tear into all the silences in our small house.

*

Songs should be sung for fights like theirs. At his worst, Camilo would grab Milo by the neck and toss him against the walls—the pictures of us all shaking themselves crooked—until he did what Camilo wanted done around the house, like mowing the lawn in the peak of the summer heat, or shovelling our snowed-in driveway during the dark winter mornings. Camilo wouldn't let Milo back into the house until he finished working. When he was finally allowed to enter, Milo skipped out on dinner, preferring to seclude himself in his room. We wouldn't see him for what seemed like days. For all his efforts, Mom always slipped a twenty for Milo under his door.

To his credit, Milo had one decent lick against our father. But first you have to understand that it was the early Nineties: gangsta rap had deeply embedded itself into every crack in the country, and LA ravaged and razed itself from the riots. Camilo stayed up late, drinking his tequila and orange juice, watching the coverage on CNN and the local news, I suppose wondering how long it would take before the fire spread to Oklahoma. One night, while Mom and I watched our shows, I heard the door across the hall open and slam against the wall.

Mom sighed. By the way her bed was positioned, we could see into Milo's room, but Camilo's broad back blocked our view. I closed my eyes to imagine what was about to happen. Camilo laid into Milo, this time on the music he thought Milo listened to—rap. He forbade Milo from buying that shit. "La musica de mayates," he called it.

"You fucking deaf or something?" Milo replied. "Can't you hear?" A few seconds later, loudly, from Milo's stereo: an echoing bang, maybe a gun or a paddle on a bare back, then the gurgled breath of a struggling man, until whips of guitars finally flood the tortured sounds.

"Putamadre," Camilo said. He grabbed the stereo and smashed it into the floor. He shut the door behind him.

*

After all this, what changed Milo's mind? What made him decide to put all that animosity aside and learn metalwork from Camilo?

"When I was young, I liked to flip through the art books at the downtown library," Milo later answered, in an interview about the aesthetics of one art influencing another. "The selection sucked, but one day I found a beat-up old book of sculptures. Jacob Epstein, Eduardo Chillida. A couple more I can't remember. The way they made the metal do what they wanted, to fit their vision. Man, an unstoppable idea shaping inflexible things—I wanted that kind of power."

*

The winter before he graduated from Capitol Hill, Milo applied to Houston's School of Art. "Honestly, on a whim," Milo answered years later, when asked about his short time in college. "I thought they'd shoot me down without hesitation. Julian Schnabel, Luis Jimenez—all those guys went to Houston. I was ready to shovel horseshit at the state fair for the rest of my life, but spend my nights making art: painting, sculpture—whatever."

Flipping through his old journals from that period, I discovered that Milo had read *CVI*, probably one of the few books he ever picked up and finished, and was influenced by Schnabel. Not by his art, but by his reputation—his absurdity, his arrogance. Superficial stuff, really: always wearing knockoff Ray-Bans he'd shoplifted from the Dollar General, even attempting to grow a patchy beard that just looked like stubborn weeds sprouting though the cracks in a pavement. It was from Schnabel's creation myth, though, that Milo stole the idea of how to distinguish himself from the other art school applicants.

On what must have been a Sunday afternoon, Milo, my mom, and I were in the kitchen. On the table, Milo had photos of his art spread out. Each one was covered by a thin plastic film, like the kind some of the boys at school used to protect their precious comics.

I inched one towards myself then eyed Milo, hopefully, so he'd let me go through his pile of photos. When he gave me a wink, I shuffled from one page to another, just as I'd do with all my favourite books. Most of them were hard to understand. Some had paint squirted on a canvas, as if Milo had squeezed a ketchup or mustard bottle too hard, and others were painted with dark colours that reminded me of a pile of leaves that turned into mushy mulch. But three photos in particular made me smile. Each one had a charcoal sketch of an armadillo rolling itself into a ball and knocking over furniture: one with a bar stool, another with a tall lamp, and the final one with a laundry hamper.

"That's you," Milo said, nodding at the armadillo, and I began to laugh. "He's named Otis, but really that's you."

Milo placed one of the flour tortillas Mom had made onto the table, set a photograph on top, then another tortilla above the photo. "¿Why are you doing that?" I asked.

"Because," he said, wrapping each bundle in a plastic Buy-4-Less bag. "I'm sending these to some people so that they'll let me into their school."

"That's stupid," I said, ducking my head to see if Mom would react to my swearing. Her movement went unchanged; she was at the counter, rolling out a ball of dough, then tossing it on one of two hot pans on the burner.

Milo sighed and shook his head. "No—that's my art."

"¿But what if *they* think it's stupid and say no?"

"Then *they* can go fuck themselves."

Mom slammed her wooden rolling pin against the ceramic tile counter.

"Sorry," he said. "Perdón."

I turned to the last photo on the table. It was of a painting. The colours—rust and coffee-stained teeth—were opaque, as if I was wearing Vaseline-covered sunglasses and all the world were vague shapes. "¿And this one?" I asked. "¿What's this one?"

"Me," Milo answered.

I examined the picture again, this time making out the pale image of Milo walking into a sheer curtain of shadows.

MARINA SANCHEZ

WALL

I will not describe those who die each year
crossing the Sonoran Desert,
from lack of water, sunstroke, wild beasts, *coyotes*.

I will not describe the desert litter
of discarded shoes, clothes, kids' backpacks,
empty plastic bottles and ladders,

the gun shell casings from the Migra,
the snorkels for swimming in the Rio Grande.
I will not question those who weave the image

of the Virgin of Guadalupe in strips
of paper through the metal posts of the wall,
so that it is visible from both sides.

I will not question the naked, female torso
painted on a teal and turquoise background,
to remember the women killed in Tijuana.

I will not describe how someone taps, raps, bangs,
hits, knocks and pounds with his hands and sticks,
on the high steel beams, the colour of dried blood.

I will not question how another has brought down
the sky and painted the beach and sea, so that
seen from afar, part of the wall will vanish.

Coyotes: smugglers of illegal immigrants
Migra: US Border Patrol

DARK EARTH

Matter Materia Mater Madre Mother

We who carry the weight of the dark earth,
remind you of your loss of reverence for her,
how we live among the sick fruits of such lack:

Materia Madre

her poisoned air and waters,
her continents strip-mined,
her forests felled.

Mater Mater

We who carry the weight of the dark earth,
remind you she is not lifeless matter,
she's not here for your God-given right

Madre Materia

to lay cement tongues that speak of your progress,
to abuse, plunder and rape her and her creatures,
she gives us life.

Mother Matter

We who carry the weight of the dark earth,
remind you she is our first mother,
when she is in pain, we all suffer.

Madre Materia

We who carry the weight of the dark earth,
remind you that you have sacrificed
our living mother for your worship of profit.

Mater Mater

We who have been carrying the weight of the dark earth,
we, sons and daughters of the corn creation myths,
whose sacred duty is to guard the earth, we ask you,

Matter Madre

when are you going to join us and take care of her?
How are you going to honour your mother?
When are you going to honour the earth?

Mother Madre Mater Materia Matter

MALINALLI REVISED

Most Mexicans call me la chingada / the damned / screwed / fucked up mother / most Mexicans vilify me as that treacherous woman / that betrayed her country to the conquistadores / ha! / how convenient! / they think Mexico would not have been conquered / if I hadn't worked for Cortes / POR FAVOR / P-L-E-A-S-E / the Spaniards had horses and firepower and were sick for gold / what did the Mexica have? / bows and arrows / and lots of gold / we all believed the prophecies / of the coming of the gods and the end of time / I was eight when my father died / then my mother remarried and sold me to another tribe / so that her son would inherit everything / if they want to blame someone / blame her / she betrayed me / I was an educated noble / then I became a slave / I had no loyalty to the tribe I came from / nor the one I was sold to nor to the Mexica / I needed to survive / but that's landed me in the blame / how convenient to say it's always the woman's fault / that she's an evil and scheming temptress / responsible for everything / what would those who must have a scapegoat / have done in my place? / I sometimes get together with some of the other bad examples of womanhood / Eve / Tiamat / Ishtar and Lilith and we try to figure out how women are both sources of life and blame / yes / they say I am a shameful and infamous whore / the founding mother of a nation of bastards by bearing Cortes' son / the first mestizo or mixed-race son of Mexico / but I wasn't the first *india* to have a child by a Spaniard / though that is the enduring narrative / most people don't know that after I bore his son / Cortes sent him to Spain and when he returned / he rejected me / his own mother / and then Cortes married me off / to one of his soldiers / I had served my purpose and he then married someone who suited him better / so / I am the twisted mother of the country / so / Mexican women are my tainted daughters / how useful for a colonial power of the mind / it's a wonder any woman rises above this mind-fuck / I do wish people would get over their 'malinchismo' / me as the stereotype for betraying the *patria* / the motherland / the guilty and treacherous one / the deceiver / I don't want thanks / but I think it's time to see me in a different light / not as victim / but as someone who responded the best way she could / to extraordinary circumstances / without complying to the traditional roles / of virgin / mother / wife and patriot / after all / how many *cabrones* have betrayed and keep betraying Mexico / but no one says a bad word about them / you know what makes me more sad than angry / that a nation with such a powerful imagination / has been stuck in this prejudice for so long /

Pero no te chinga! *Fucks me off it does*

KARINA LICKORISH QUINN

THE WALLS OF GRINGO BUCKMAN

LIKE THE FRESH pink skin under a scab, but all over – that was Gringo Buckman. Permanently peeling. Even the half-hearted winter sun, filtered through the Limenian neblina, was enough to scrape away the top layers of his flesh and leave him shiny and raw, like a hermit crab caught out of its shell. El cangrejo Buckman. Yes, Crabby Buckman we should have called him. It might have stuck, too, what with his furtiveness, his scuttling away sideways whenever he saw us coming.

He was a suspicious man – suspicious of us, I mean. *We* were never wary of *him* – more intrigued. Intrigued the way a child is about furtive crawling things. Just as eagerly as we thrust our hands into the sand to unearth sand fleas or hacked with spades to crack mussels from the rocks, yes, with all that same reckless, boisterous, childish curiosity of gutting still-living fish and throwing cancha at the seabirds, we circled the house of Gringo Buckman and longed to mine him like a precious stone. To crack open his shell and tear him, a glistening pinkish pearl, out.

But we were not the reason for the old man's walls: those ramparts were entirely his own invention. He built them, first, in his own mistrustful mind, convinced beyond doubt of a thousand dangers beyond the borders of his patch of land on the corner of Calle Arica and Enrique Meiggs. Ladrones. Narcos. Guerillas with machetes. Every kind of bad hombre was, in Buckman's intoxicating fantasy of victimhood, lurking on the sidewalk outside his door. In reality, it was just us: the chiquillos of the neighbourhood, scuttling back and forth from school, woollen socks baggy around our ankles, smears of vanilla ice cream sandwich across our faces. But in the mind of Old Man Buckman, Miraflores was crawling with dangers.

How did the viejo come to be stranded in Lima so far from home, terrorised among people that so unnerved him, like a white rabbit among scorpions? He must have come, I suppose, with some business. Some North American company, mining guano, drilling for oil or trawling for Peruvian anchoveta and then, when the investors withdrew after the junta, he was forgotten and left behind, human jetsam, bleached by the sun, bloated by saltwater, thrown ashore by the tide and abandoned. Abandoned alone. He did not seem to have any gringo friends. No Peruvian friends either. He lived a solitary life. A life of routine and simple pleasures.

He did not always hide behind the walls. There was a time, a time pre-ramparts, when he could be spotted out in the city, taking a copa at El Haiti, strolling along El Malecón or sitting in the Parque Kennedy, flat cap on his speckled head, crumpled linen jacket sagging from his shoulders – that is how I remember him most, hunched on a bench in the shade of flame trees, the street-children huddling around him, peddling lemon candies or Chiclets or plastic icons of Sarita Colonia and warbling *Señor, señor, una monedita* and he, rustling the pages of his Wall Street Journal in vexation or swatting at the swarm with his walking stick, shouting *¡Vete! ¡Vete!*

Even before he interred himself, alive, behind those walls of razor wire and concrete, he had no patience for either poverty or youth. If, walking along the pavement, he met with a group of us, children of the barrio, coming towards him he would thrust out his walking stick like a sword and slice it back and forth through the air so that we would part, like the Red Sea before Moses, keen to avoid the slashes of its shaft against our legs. Even now, all these years later, I wear on my shins scars of the stick of Gringo Buckman.

When we gathered on his lawn, huddling around the bucayo tree to peer into his windows or wait for his maid, Teresita, to emerge and distribute among us the imported

American candies that she smuggled out from his kitchen, he would shout down at us from his window and pelt us with ice cubes the same way that our mothers pelted the stray, rabid dogs that cocked their legs over the alstroemeria or deposited steaming piles of shit among the geraniums. He cursed us in English with a string of sounds and expletives that meant nothing to us, and he called all the girls 'Maria' and all the boys 'Juan'. We all looked the same to him, I suppose, never mind that Marisol had eyes almost as green as his or that Ana-Paula had a scar on her cheek shaped like a gull over water. I suppose he never noticed that Enrique's hair curled like corkscrews whereas Julio's fell over his eyes like a veil of black silk or that Diana's ears were pointed, elfish, and Dieguito had only one thumb. To him, we were replicates: copies of some original cast, identical – paper dolls cut from the same sheet and then divided and set loose on the city. I imagine that in his nightmares he saw us as living facsimiles, indistinguishable and endless, pouring forth, copy after copy, from some inexhaustible printing press – a legion of Juans and Marias to flood to his front yard, press their sticky little bodies against his door and eyeball him through the key hole.

As much as we appalled him, we yearned for him to love us – not collectively, as a horde, but individually and exclusively. We cast him in the role of Daddy Warbucks in our childish fantasies in which we would sit on his knee eating Lay's chips and candy floss and then he would whisk us away on the Good Ship Lollipop to his mansion north of el Río Bravo, where life would be easy and carefree. Where, perhaps, he would dote on Atacama skin and beetle-black hair the way our own abuelos doted on the wheaten curls and lizard green eyes of the nenita from the commercials for Gloria milk.

But Gringo Buckman had no interest in adopting us as surrogate grandbabies. The only interest he showed was in the vedettes of the chicha press, the nubile young calatas on the front pages of Ajá and Trome, over which he would run his eyes slowly – too slowly for public decency – as he stood, leaning heavily on his stick, in front of the tobacconist's stand. The burnished pecan breasts, thighs and haunches of those pages, of the Misses Venezuela in particular, were not – or did not seem to be – anathema to him, nor were the writhing bodies of the young lovers necking in the Parque del Amor, whom he watched intently, wistfully, as if they reminded him of a great thing lost.

Un viejo verde. That is what they called him, especially the ladies of the barrio, the mothers, aunties, the sisters from the convent. *A green old creep*. Green. Not ripe. Not yet matured, sexually speaking. A lech. And, in a way, it was this – his lechery, his pirópería – that was his downfall. Those intoxicating sirens of the chicha press drew him to his doom for, as he perused the bodies of the café-con-leche women melted across the pages of those red top tabloids, his eyes were drawn, eventually, inevitably, to the salacious headlines, which – even with his scanty Spanish – he could understand were dripping with threat and bad blood. It was these headlines that poisoned his mind against us, convincing him of the truthfulness of the nightmares they peddled – of drug cartels burrowing below his feet and bubonic plague bubbling in every drainpipe and senderistas with machetes lurking in wait around every turn.

So we were not the reason for the walls of Gringo Buckman. It was the illusory terror of the crónica roja that caused the old man to lose his mind – to see in our faces semblances of assassins and thieves – and then to bury himself alive.

It started with the wrought ironwork: black bars like cages over the windows and, later, the door, fortified with a collection of padlocks and deadbolts. Simply to enter the house, Teresita needed a bundle of keys the size of a grapefruit that hung so heavily from her belt that it sagged down over her right hip and made her limp as she walked. After the bars came the fences, chain link, erected at the perimeter of his land, dividing lawn from pavement, neighbour from neighbour, us from Buckman. No longer could we congregate around el Gringo's bucayo tree. Instead, we lined up at the fences, hooked our fingers through the holes and squeezed our faces against the wires, pressing their imprint onto our cheeks. On tiptoe, we strained to catch a glimpse of the old man through the cracks in his blinds, for he had stopped coming out and, as market forces instruct us, his scarcity had deepened our demand. Occasionally, only very occasionally, he emerged, squinting against the sun, shuffling around the yard with crooked back to pick up the garbage that blew through the fence and out of the reach of the municipal road sweepers. Over the months of his confinement, he had withered and his hands had succumbed to the gnarling of age: with fingers locked together, moving in unison opposite a hooked thumb, his hands were crustacean pincers with which he scooped up the detritus from the lawn.

Then he sacked Teresita. She emerged one afternoon, frantic, the tip of the old man's stick in the small of her back; he scuffling behind in his fleece-lined house shoes hollering at her, *¡Impostora! ¡Impostora!*, she scraping the tears from her cheeks with her fists, denuded of her globe of keys. Out of the gate he shoved her and then scuttled back into his fortress, accompanied by the chiming and clicking of bolts and springs, latches locking into place.

That was a blow for us because our supply of American snacks – chips by Pringle, Kisses Hershey, boxes of Mike y Ike – ran dry. It was an even greater blow for Teresita who, finding herself without work, disappeared from our neighbourhood, from our lives, entirely until, some months later, my mother and I spotted her selling avocados from a cart on the Óvalo Gutierrez.

After the excommunication of Teresita came the impenetrable walls, constructed with blocks of cement piled two storeys high by a five-man team who worked around the clock for three days during my school's summer vacation. From my window, I watched the labourers peeling down to their glistening walnut skin, dripping with perspiration under the relentless summer sun. I was too young – perhaps only a few months too young – for them to inspire in me any feeling other than idle curiosity, but I watched them all day as they worked for the Gringo while he barked orders at them in English from his bedroom window: "You! Come! Closer... Closer... Stop! Right there! That's right! Faster! Faster!" Block by block, the dusty grey walls grew until Buckman's house, brutalist and stark as the Museo de la Nación, squatted in shadow, dingy and sad against the lúcuma yellows and cactus greens of the neighbouring neo-colonial casas of Calle Arica.

Once those walls were erected, no one came in or out of the old man's home. No gardeners. No cleaners. There were no visits from anybody of any kind. His food was delivered in a wooden crate through a mechanised hatch of corrugated iron in the wall, operated via an intercom system with a one-way camera. He was cut off. Disconnected. Utterly marooned within the ramparts of his concrete isle. They say he had no phone. No television. Not even a radio. That's what they say. His only connection to the outside world was through the newspapers that were delivered daily, lobbed by the mailman over his walls. I imagine him, still, sat at his table, poring over those tabloids with a magnifying glass and a dictionary, getting light-headed from bingeing on the terror poured forth by the chicha press.

The summer that Gringo Buckman inhumed himself I spent at Ana-Paula's house, playing Jacks and eating sandwiches of Bimbo bread with margarine and sugar up on the flat roof where we could look down into the Sevillian patio at the centre of Buckman's house. There, we waited, hoping to see his hairless head emerge and glow neon pink in the sunlight. We saw him a few times, shuffling across the azulejo tiles in a flannel night-robe and slippers, and each time we added a strike to our tally chart of chalk on the parapet. We conjectured whether we could fashion a pulley system by which we could deliver him parcels – things we would miss if sentenced to solitary confinement for the rest of our lives: handwritten notes, portions of pastél de choclo, Karamanduka bread. It was on a day that we were leaning over the parapet and plotting how we would construct such a system that el viejo Buckman emerged and, with his hand positioned as a shield against the sun, squinted up at us with his bright lime eyes. For a moment, we were spellbound, watching him watching us. Then we squealed, fell to the ground, clutched our hands over our heads and lay there giggling together.

By the following morning, the old man had stretched a tarpaulin sheet over the patio, nailed it into the four surrounding walls, and boxed himself in, hidden from our sight entirely. The week after, the tops of his walls were embellished with shards of glass and rolls of razor wire. Not even the pigeons trespassed there then.

Over the years we forgot about el Gringo. We grew, graduated from school, married; some of us, the chiquillos of the barrio, emigrated, leaving for the land north of the Río Bravo or for Europe. The old casonas of Miraflores were sold, priced by the square metre, demolished, replaced by apartment complexes in the North American style where most of the residents were newcomers who had never known about old crustacean Buckman. We grew blind to the box of grey concrete on the corner of Calles Arica y Meiggs from which no one emerged and into which no one ventured.

Until, one summer, more than a decade later, we caught a whiff of something – dead fish and past-it fruit. Faint at first – a little sweet, a little rotten – the initial guffs that came and went with the breeze did not perturb us. In Lima, we are accustomed to smells, evanescent flatulations of the sea that break across the city and then dissipate. So, for a few days, we ignored the new fragrance, continued life more or less as normal, perhaps doused ourselves with a little more agua de colonia or boiled some cinnamon in water on the stove.

But the odour, rather than departing, intensified. We were driven almost mad by it. We rifled through our homes, scoured our trash, searching for a source. When our excavations proved fruitless, we blamed one another, pointed fingers, whispered behind our hands about our neighbours' hygiene. When the stench reached an apocalyptic intensity, as pestilent on the rooftops as in the streets, as acrid indoors as out, inescapable and unmaskable, then we reunited, clubbing together to pay for drain investigations and pest controllers. We petitioned the municipality of Miraflores for the sewers to be inspected and the gutters to be sluiced. We collaborated in task forces to comb the flower borders, foraging for festering deposits of dog shit or putrid carcasses. But, for all our efforts, the stinking plague still crept through our barrio.

I don't know to whom it occurred to lay the culpa on the old forgotten plot at the corner. Everyone likes to claim the idea was his own. I was not there when it happened. I was sleeping, fitfully, retching between dreams, a napkin soaked in eucalyptus and neroli laid across my face. I know about the discovery only from things that I am told. And they tell me the serenazgo was called in the dead of night. They tell me how the guards rang and rang at the intercom, entirely in vain. They say that the firemen were summoned to break into the house with a crowbar, to slice the padlocks with enormous bolt cutters and hack off the mortise locks with an axe. Even then, the door had become so swollen, so warped from years of disuse, that the wood had fused to the frame and had to be battered down by three strong men together. And, all the time they worked, they wore scarves tied around their faces to shield themselves from the pestiferous odour of decay that the house exhaled. And the neighbours gathered on the sidewalk to watch the forced penetration of the stronghold of Buckman under the veil of darkness.

I arrived the next day not out of voyeuristic curiosity but plainly and simply because I was the doctor closest to the scene qualified to certify deaths. Though I will admit, and without shame, that I took my time walking through that house, examining the way that Gringo Buckman had lived inside that concrete shell into which he had insinuated himself and disappeared. So many years without Teresita, without domestic assistance of any kind, had taken their toll: the thick Limenian dust had gathered in ankle-high trenches along the inner walls and coated every item of furniture with a veil of grey ash. The shameless city birds, winged rats, had found a way to break inside and, once there, found themselves trapped, splattering their panic in livid purple and yellow faeces on every surface, horizontal and vertical, and then died and landed, spread-eagled, wherever they fell. Out in the Sevillian patio, where the sun cast slashes of light through the shredded tarpaulin, nature had invaded. Weeds, robust and brawny with monster tendrils like swollen limbs, had burst through the ground, buckling the tiles and stretching across the azulejo rubble like squids crawling up from the underworld. One had crept, with an undulating vine as thick as a man's neck, up a wall and into the old man's bedroom where it had broken a hole in the window and emerged the other side, winding its way across the front lawn, trampling the bucayo tree, stretching on towards the front gate like a giant Amazonian snake. Under the crumbling arches of the loggia, stacks of newspapers, bleached by the sun, dampened and moulding from years of humidity, leaned against each other, exhausted. I had the impression that, if I touched them, they would explode into a cloud of flakes and dust. Years of stories and scandals scattered as powder by a gust of air.

El Gringo Buckman was at the back of the house where the air was thick and nauseous and buzzed with a pall of flies. They had left him as they found him. No one had dared to touch the old man – what was left of him – so I found him undisturbed, emaciated and crumpled at the bottom of the stairs, his face pressed against the dusty flagstones, twisted neck, skin a jaundiced pink, like that of a plucked chicken, but pockmarked where maggots had burrowed in. I examined the body, confirmed (though it was hardly necessary) that the old man was dead, concluded that he had fallen, tripped on a step and plummeted, probably all the way from the first floor, but had not died in the instant: on the balance of probabilities he had lain there several days and what finished him was the dehydration. His fort had become his sepulchre.

Whoever shared the details of the old man's degradation, it was not me: professional discretion restrained me from broadcasting the depths to which he had fallen, but still the tabloids managed to plaster their pages the next day with pictures of the crumpled old man lying in the dirt. There was a close up of his face, only half-heartedly pixelated, and one high resolution shot of his bloated, yellowing hand lying next to a gleaming mahogany brown cockroach. Even El Comercio dedicated half a page to the story alongside an advertisement for portable panic alarms for the elderly and infirm.

We learned, in the coming weeks, that old Buckman had children – a middle-aged son and daughter who flew down to take care of his estate. I met them only once, when I visited them at the house to express my condolences (in which they showed little interest) and to give them my invoice for the certification of death. They greeted me with brisk handshakes and pursed lips, the son directing his attention primarily to his cellular phone, the daughter rubbing the palms of her hands up and down her arms as if she felt a chill, though it was almost midday in midsummer. Her nails were lacquered in a frosty pink that matched the kitten heels she wore, and she had a habit of lifting first one shoe then the other off the floor and shivering her feet from the ankle as if to shake off the dust, all the time with a faraway look that glazed her eyes with cataracts of apathy. Behind her legs hid a little girl of maybe six or seven, a grand-daughter, I supposed, to Gringo Buckman. From behind her Shirley Temple curls two feline eyes of avocado green watched me, fixated.

The Buckman children took nothing with them when they left – no mementos of the old man, no photographs for posterity. The patch of land was put up for speedy sale and, within days, the demolition men arrived with a wrecking ball to raze the entire plot. I watched its first swing – witnessed the tremulous arc it made through the air and the crack that split the first wall diagonally like a lightning bolt. By that evening, all the homes on the block had been gilded with a fine layer of the soot that had mushroomed apocalyptically from the building ground.

The demolition was quick, but it took weeks for the municipality to attend to the pile of Buckman's furniture left out on the sidewalk. It was evident that nothing of his had been worth selling: all of the wood had been infested with woodworm; the upholstery, stained by years of damp, was discoloured; the dust, empowered by the humidity, had burrowed and solidified in every groove and crevice. Worst of all, the smell of death had penetrated deep into every fibre. So everything had been tossed out onto the pavement to await collection by the garbage men – only, the garbage men never came. Stray dogs urinated on the stinking heap. Rats scurried in and out, thankful for shelter from the sun's glare. The occasional passer-by stopped to assess whether anything could be salvaged – nothing was touched by human hands. The stench repelled even the neediest of scavengers.

Eventually, tired of waiting for the city garbage men, someone set fire to the redolent heap. It was late evening and the blaze lit up the neighbourhood, gleaming through our windows, casting flickering shadows on our walls. It drew us out of our homes and into the streets. We all, new residents and old, came out to watch the pyre burn, transfixed by how the ochre flames danced and licked the livid sky, our faces illuminated, each one a golden sun against the night.

INTERVIEW

X NATHALIE TEITLER
GAËL LE CORNEC

NT: my first question is about identity, how do you define your identity?

Gaël: Yes, I believe identity shifts according to where you are in your life and who you are surrounded by: when I'm with my Brazilian friends I become Brazilian, with my French friends I become quite French. It shifts as well depending on how you choose to represent yourself in that moment. In addition to that, I am a multiplicity of backgrounds; my DNA test shows that I am a hybrid, I have 12 ethnicities in me! I am of indigenous, white and black heritage. But at the same time, even if I was born in the Amazon, I found myself feeling much more Latin American when I left Brazil. You suddenly look at yourself from a distance and realise how connected you are to your birthplace and to that part of the world.

NT: Let's talk a little bit about you as an artist; you are a successful playwright, actor, director and I know you have other strings to your bow. How much would you consider your Latinx identity has impacted on your art? For example, when I read through your plays there was some experimentation in the way you use language and it was highly political. That seemed to tie in very well with Latin American traditions of literature/ theatre.

Gaël: I guess as a writer you try to write the truth of what is inside of you and how you perceive the world: it will always be an amalgamation of your identity and your culture and the cultures you share and take part in. I think it is probably the job of the reader/audience to pick out the similarities with other artists, to say that there are parallels or influences. But yeah, being of multiple heritage does influence the way I express myself; I think the way we express ourselves is complex and fluid, it shifts according to the story you are telling. One constant, however, is that my stories always centre on female characters, and most of the time under-represented female characters.

NT: Can you explain a little bit about the tradition of Latin American theatre in the UK?

Gaël: It's still an emerging tradition. Before CASA Latin American Theatre Festival, there was no organisation solely dedicated to Latin American theatre in the UK. I worked with CASA for 8 years and was the international programmer for a while; it gave me the opportunity to travel to Latin America and bring work over here to British audiences. I feel CASA developed a cycle of bringing theatre that has influenced a whole generation of playwrights and theatre-makers in the UK. CASA has also given space to the Latinx theatre makers who were here to develop their work. We had a programme for emerging London based Latinx theatre makers to present a 15-minute piece on a scratch night. Some of those pieces went on to become full shows, went to the Edinburgh Fringe and won awards. That started placing Latinx theatre makers (playwrights, actors, directors) in the spotlight.

NT: I read the article you wrote in a writing commission you did for the British Council; you talked about the prejudices and stereotypes that exist around Latin actors. What experiences have you had?

Gaël: When I first moved here and started my acting career, I was automatically placed in the category of the 'hot Latina', even by my agents. I realised that this was how Latin Americans, especially women, were stereotyped. I think it is changing now but the constant labelling of that stereotype did annoy me in my early career. I actually wonder where that comes from in the UK.

NT: Perhaps some of the stereotypes come from how Latin Americans are presented in North American popular culture and that has filtered through to the UK. It's also probably a misunderstanding based on the dance and music, the Carnival culture, that is so popular here. There is also the distance from Latin America in that it was never a British colony so the culture is very removed and everything is mediated through other colonisers/ world powers.

Gaël: Yes, people see the Carnival culture and forget that is just one time of the year, one aspect of the culture but the perception is of exuberance and physical and sexual freedom so the political side of it is completely lost.

NT: In turbulent times, the Western market dictates the mainstream cultural product to some extent.

Gaël: I'm wondering if the stereotypes also come from the need to try and understand another culture; if it makes it easier to process and categorise what that culture is. So by labelling Latin American culture as 'hot' it becomes contained in a way.

NT: And they haven't replaced the stereotype yet with the more complex and politically active reality of the women of this culture. Western people are always surprised when they learn of the long history of feminism in Latin America.

Finally, I wanted to ask you something about the political/ activist side of your work. What is interesting is that every single British Latinx writer I have spoken to has really strong political and often similar views, and almost all are activists both in their art and outside it.

Gaël: For me it comes from growing up in the Amazon and being surrounded by conflict, violence and genocide. Somehow the narratives I choose to tell are charged with that, with this violence I witnessed in my childhood. Children raised in that part of the world are exposed to things no child should ever see or hear. I'm lucky to be an artist and able to transform trauma into story.

NT: Many of the other British Latinx artists I have spoken to also use silence and coding in their work – whether it is poetry, fiction, theatre or dance.

Gaël: Yes, I do as well. Silence for me is not an absence of words, it's when words are not enough. It's when the space is so charged that there are no words to describe it. The silences I write into my plays carry meaning, they are the subtext of a scene, they outline what's really going on. For example, in *Camille Claudel*, there is a whole silent scene, no dialogues, just a description of the internal psychological state of the main character. It's for the actor to interpret that state, without a word, just with their presence and actions on stage. In *The Other*, I challenged myself to write without following the rules of 'theatre writing', using imagery, silences and metaphors. The extract in this anthology is an example of writing metaphorically.

NT: The last thing I wanted to ask you is about different audiences. When you perform in front of a Brazilian audience, for example, is there a significant difference in the way the work is received?

Gaël: It depends on the work. When I performed my piece

Efemera, a play about violence against Brazilian women in London I didn't want it to be just for a Brazilian audience. I wanted British audiences to know, this was actually happening. So I had two actors on stage: one British and one Brazilian because I wanted the audience to see through the lenses of both, feel empathy towards both characters and understand that domestic violence can happen to anyone regardless of culture. It's not just something that happens to women 'over there' in that community.

We performed *Efemera* here at the Southwark Playhouse and it felt very much like a British theatre audience. Then we performed in Brazil in the favela da Maré in Rio de Janeiro and the response was different: the audience was incredibly lively and warm and at the end of the play there were all these women coming up to us to tell their own stories. That's when we realised that if we were going to do this again we needed to set up a support network for these women. That's when the work fully embraces the cause it is portraying and becomes even more activist.

In *The Other,* which I mentioned earlier, the piece featured in this anthology, I consciously wanted to create a one woman play that any audience member from anywhere in the world would watch and go 'yes, we have to help refugee children'. And to try to reach that universality I didn't write it like a traditional theatre piece. It is mostly told through imagery and poetic language. By choosing that more experimental path I also wanted to push the boundaries of what theatre can do.

NT: Yes, art can be the beginning of a conversation that reaches into the community and shows that there are different ways of doing things, ways of healing and change and that seems to be present in Latinx art in the UK and in the States. It's a fundamental part of our art.

AUTHOR BIOGRAPHIES

Juana Adcock

Juana Adcock is a poet, translator and performer working in English and Spanish. She was born in Mexico in 1982 and has lived in Glasgow since 2007. Her translations and poems on language, communication, migration, identity and violence have appeared in numerous publications such as *Magma Poetry*, *Shearsman*, *Asymptote*, the *LitHub* and *Words Without Borders*, among others. Her first book, *Manca*, explores the anatomy of violence in the Mexican drug war and was named by *Reforma*'s distinguished critic Sergio González Rodríguez as one of the best books published in 2014. In 2016 she was named one of the 'Ten New Voices from Europe' by Literary Europe Live and the organization Literature Across Frontiers, and she has performed at numerous literary festivals internationally. Her English language debut, *Split* (Blue Diode Press, 2019) was awarded the Poetry Book Society Winter Choice for 2019.

Leo Boix

Leo Boix is a Latinx bilingual poet, translator and journalist born in Argentina who lives and works in the UK. Boix has published two poetry collections in Spanish, *Un lugar propio* (2015) and *Mar de noche* (2017), and has been included in many anthologies, such as *Ten: Poets of the New Generation* (Bloodaxe), *Why Poetry* (Verve Poetry Press) and *Islands Are But Mountains: Contemporary Poetry from Great Britain* (Platypus Press). His poems have appeared in POETRY, PN Review, The Poetry Review, Modern Poetry in Translation, The Manchester Review, The White Review, Letras Libres, Magma Poetry, The Rialto, The Morning Star, SouthBank Poetry and elsewhere. Boix is a fellow of The Complete

Works Program and co-director of Invisible Presence, an Arts Council England national scheme to nurture new voices of Latinx writers in the UK. He is a board member of Magma Poetry, co-editor of its Resistencia issue showcasing the best Latin American and Latinx writing, and an advisory board member of the Poetry Translation Centre in London. Boix is the recipient of the Keats-Shelley Prize 2019. His debut English collection will be out in 2021 with Chatto & Windus.

Armando Celayo

Armando Celayo (Chicanx) received an M.A. in Creative Writing from the University of East Anglia. His work has been published in *Ambit, PEN International,* and *Huizache,* among several other places, and has won numerous awards including the Salt Prize for Best Individual Flash Fiction and a grant from Arts Council England. He is working on two books, *For the Recovery of Lost Things,* a novel-in-stories, and *Downward Is Heavenward,* a novel.

Gaël Le Cornec

Born in the Amazon, Gaël's fascination for theatre started as a child when reading plays at night by candlelight.

After graduating with a BA in Biology at the University of São Paulo, Gaël trained as an actor at the Grotowski Institute (Poland) and the Meisner Ruskin School of Acting (Los Angeles). She holds a Masters in Cultural & critical studies from Birkbeck University in London and attended the Royal Court Programme for emerging writers in 2009. Fluent in 4 languages: English, French, Portuguese and Spanish, her acting credits include 23 stage productions around the world including the one-woman shows *The Other, The last days of Gilda, Camille Claudel and Frida Kahlo: Viva La vida!.* Writing credits include the plays *The Broken Clock, Kitchen, The Late Hour, Under the skin* and *Camille Claudel.* Gaël has worked in various capacity for companies such as Secret Cinema, the Royal Shakespeare Company, Company of Angels, Two Gents and Theatre Sans Frontieres.

Maia Elsner

Maia Elsner was born in London to a Mexican mother, and a Jewish father, whose parents fled Poland as refugees from the Holocaust. She grew up between Oxford and Mexico City, where most of her family still live, with stints spent in France and Italy. Maia began writing poetry while studying race, migration and incarceration in the US and while tutoring English language and literature in a medium-maximum security prison in Massachusetts. Her work investigates the struggles of belonging and survival in the space between intergenerational trauma and the possibility of hope. Her writing about migration explores the violences of colonial expansion and persecution, the laws that seek to limit and define what it means to be human, and resistance to categorization, the potentiality, always, of expanding boundaries, of transcending and transformation. Maia's poems have appeared in a variety of places, both online and in print, in British, American and Canadian journals, including *Colorado Review, Blackbox Manifold, The Missouri Review, Willow Springs* and *The Ekphrastic Review*. She now lives in South London.

Katherine Lockton

At a very young age, Katherine fell from a very high window. Although poorly remembered, the incident has had a subconscious influence on much of her later work, which explores emotional and intellectual aspects of falling in a spiritual or metaphysical sense. Writing in Spanish and English, her writing is heavily influenced by being bilingual, having a dual heritage and the customs, culture, history, people and politics of Bolivia.
Katherine has won a number of awards including the Inaugural International Travel Bursary by The Saltire Society and British Council Scotland, shortlisted for Girton College's Jane Martin Poetry Prize, and won first place in the Field Poetry Competition judged by Martin Figura. She co-edited (with Carlo Pirozzi) an anthology of new Scottish war poems 'Like Leaves in Autumn' published by Luath Press.
Her poems have been published in *The Glasgow Review of Books*, *Northwords Now*, *Magma*, *Poem magazine*, *The Spectator*, *PN Review* and *Ink, Sweat and Tears* and her work was recently nominated for the Forward Prize for best poem by *Magma* and *The Spectator*.

Patrizia Longhitano

Patrizia Longhitano was born in Brazil and lived in Manaus until she was eight years old. She moved to Italy with her adoptive parents until 2005 when she decided to move to the UK. Since then, she has been living in London working as a nanny. She started writing poems in English more than ten years ago. Some of her poems have appeared in *Rialto*, *South Bank Poetry* and *The Delinquent*.

Karina Lickorish Quinn

Karina Lickorish Quinn is a Peruvian-British writer who grew up between the English Midlands, Lima and New York. She now lives in London with her husband and her two beloved cats. In a past life, Karina was a family law barrister and then a secondary school teacher. She now teaches creative writing at the University of Leeds, where she is the Teaching Fellow in Creative Writing, and Queen Mary University of London, where she is also completing her PhD. Her work thus far has primarily explored migration, transnationalism and identity as well as motherhood and the female experience. Her short story 'Oögenesis' was short-listed for The White Review short story prize in 2016. She has published work in various literary journals including *The Offing*, the *Journal of Latina Critical Feminism* and *Question Journal*. Karina writes in and between English, Spanish and Spanglish and is passionate about writing that erases boundaries between languages: her bilingual short story 'Spanglish' was published by *Asymptote Journal* and she has conducted research into teaching translingual writing in the primary and secondary classroom. She is currently editing her debut novel and hopes to share it with the world in the not too-distant future..

Marina Sanchez

Marina is a Latinish mix of Native American/Spanish/British and an award-winning poet and translator, widely published in literary journals including *The Shop, South Bank Poetry, Acumen, Obsessed with Pipework*, and *The Reader* magazine as well as online with *Anima Press, Second Light, Scintilla, Stand* and *Nutshell*. Her poems have also been longlisted, shortlisted and finalists in several Cinnamon Press competitions. She contributed to the anthologies *In Protest: 150 Poems for Human Rights* (now reprinted) and *Beautiful Cadaver* (2019). Marina's pamphlet *Dragon Child* (Acumen, 2014), was Book of the Month on the Poetry Kit website and she was selected for the Invisible Presence Project promoting British Latinx writers.

Luiza Sauma

Luiza Sauma was born in Rio de Janeiro and emigrated to London with her family when she was four years old – initially for two years, but they never left. She is the author of two novels, *Flesh and Bone and Water* (2017) and *Everything You Ever Wanted* (2019), both published by Viking. The latter was described by Rachel Seiffert in the *Guardian* as "wry and frequently beautiful, and its culmination is surprising and deeply moving" and by the *i* as "a haunting examination of depression and anxiety rendered in diamond-sharp prose". Luiza studied English at the University of Leeds before becoming a journalist. She worked at the *Independent on Sunday* for several years and has also written for the *Guardian*, the *Telegraph*, the *i*, *Five Dials* and others. She has an MA in Creative and Life Writing from Goldsmiths, University of London, where she won the Pat Kavanagh Award.

AFTERWORD

THE UN NUEVO Sol anthology is just the first step in getting British Latinx representation onto mainstream UK and global literature platforms. I recognise that there are very important sectors of the community: Afro Latinx, Asian Latinx, disabled Latinx that are not currently represented. These groups are incredibly important and the lack of inclusion is down to the fact that when a project of this size is undertaken by two individuals (Leo Boix and I), sadly the results will be necessarily imperfect. In the two years of extensive searches across community networks and at grassroots level we have not yet found writers from these groups, but we will and they will be celebrated. The goal is to get a foot in the door and to open up opportunities for everyone in the future. I hope that by publishing this anthology, British Latinx writers from all sectors are emboldened to come forward and join us at readings and further publications. I urge them to get in touch and I will continue to work to create structures of support and development across the British Latinx community so that we can all move together in solidarity.

NATHALIE TEITLER